DARK MOON

When her aunt dies, Jemima is offered a home with her stern uncle, but vows to make her own way in the world by working at a coaching inn. She falls for the handsome and fascinating Giles Morton, but he has a menacing secret that could endanger them both. When Jemima is forced to choose between her own safety and saving the man she loves, she doesn't hesitate for a moment — but will they both come out of it alive?

CATRIONA McCUAIG

DARK
MOON

Complete and Unabridged

LINFORD
Leicester

First published in Great Britain in 2007

First Linford Edition
published 2007

British Library CIP Data

McCuaig, Catriona
    Dark moon.—Large print ed.—
Linford romance library
    1. Love stories
    2. Large type books
    I. Title
    823.9′2 [F]

    ISBN 978–1–84782–036–5

Published by
F. A. Thorpe (Publishing)
Anstey, Leicestershire

Set by Words & Graphics Ltd.
Anstey, Leicestershire
Printed and bound in Great Britain by
T. J. International Ltd., Padstow, Cornwall

This book is printed on acid-free paper

1

Jemima Coates winced as the coach hit yet another pothole in the road. The journey from London to Bedford was turning into a nightmare. The vehicle had been designed to carry six passengers but the coachman had given in to the pleas of a harassed young mother with a fretful three-year old, who said that the boy could sit on her lap, so they were seven in number.

If only the child had behaved nicely, Jemima mourned, rubbing her throbbing head, it would have been all right, but he had spent the last hour on his feet, pushing his way from one passenger to another before breaking into a furious wailing which his mother had been unable to control. He had finally fallen asleep with his thumb in his mouth and his exhausted parent was now bent over his curly head, trying to get some rest before he woke up again.

'Going far, are you?' Jemima's neighbour was unpacking a substantial snack and offered her a corner of mutton pie, which was gratefully accepted.

'All the way,' Jemima admitted. 'All the way to Bedford; that's if we ever get there! How long is it supposed to take, anyway?'

'Eleven hours, counting stops along the way. A bit much, isn't it? Never mind, I've made this trip before, and unless I'm very much mistaken we'll be stopping soon, at the sign of the Angel. I'm thirsting for a nice hot cup of tea.'

A cup of tea sounded like a gift from heaven, but Jemima hoped fervently that there wasn't a long queue at the privy, because she was feeling desperate. Perhaps if she rudely elbowed her way off the coach the moment it stopped it would be all right. Her companion was watching her, bright-eyed.

'On leave from service, are you, and

going home to see your family?'

'In a way.' Jemima thought of dear Aunt Mab, whose burial had recently taken place in the churchyard across from Sparrow Street, where they had been living. Mab was her father's sister, who had taken care of Jemima ever since her parents had died from cholera when she was three years old.

Mab received a pension from her soldier son which enabled them to live in modest comfort in a rented terraced house, sharing the work of the household and occasionally taken in sewing to make a little extra money for luxuries.

Now Mab was gone, and Jemima was on her way to stay with her mother's brother, who was a cooper at Bedford. She explained this to the older woman.

'Aunt Dorcas has twelve children, all under sixteen, so she'll be glad of the help, Uncle Josh says.'

'Dearie me! But surely the older girls lend a hand?'

Jemima pulled a face. 'The first seven are all boys.'

'And we all know how useless lads can be! The poor soul will have you running about from morn until night, if I know anything about it! But your uncle is a cooper, you say? A good trade, that. There's always a need for casks and barrels. But doesn't your aunt have a little maid or two as it is?'

'I think he hired a girl when Auntie had the twins, but he says she won't be needed any more now I'm coming.'

By the expression on the woman's face Jemima knew they shared the same opinion of Joshua Burnett. Thrifty, or careful, was the polite term. Downright mean was what any sensible person would have said.

Jemima was young and strong and not afraid of hard work, but she did wonder how she would get on in the Burnett household. She had been spoiled, growing up under Aunt Mab's kindly supervision, and now she was about to see how the other half lived.

'Here we are at the Angel!' her seat mate observed with satisfaction, putting her bonnet back on and tying the strings in a firm bow. The stagecoach drew to a stop in a wide yard, and Jemima hopped off the minute the door opened.

'Here, steady on, you'll have me over!' the driver grunted, but she flashed him a quick smile and kept going.

A tall young man was crossing the yard with a brimming water bucket in each hand. In her headlong flight Jemima just had time to notice that he was quite handsome in a rugged sort of way, with brown curly hair and dark eyes.

'Which way to the . . . ' she panted.

'That green door down yonder,' he shouted, before she had time to finish her request. Embarrassed, she kept going, reflecting that the people who worked here must be used to such questions.

That brief glimpse of the ostler, or

whatever he was, had intrigued Jemima and when she entered the inn she looked around her, hoping to see him again, but he was nowhere in sight. As an outside worker he probably slept over the stables and ate his meals in the kitchen. She chided herself for being foolish. She had many miles to travel and would never see the man again, so what was the point in starting up a casual conversation?

The public rooms were filled with people, not only her fellow travellers, but others as well, standing guard over a variety of baggage. No doubt they were waiting for a coach or coaches going in the other direction. The landlord, if that's who he was, was doing a brisk trade in tankards of beer, while a young woman of about Jemima's age was moving about the room with a tray of pies, bread and cheese, which soon disappeared into the customers' eager hands.

Seeing her friend from the coach, Jemima pushed her way through the crowd and sank down beside her.

'There's a pot of tea on its way, m'dear! I'm sure you'll be glad of one. I'm that parched! I must have swallowed a pound of dust on that road.'

'I'm more hungry than anything,' Jemima admitted. 'Are they serving food as well?'

'At a price! These places always charge twice as much as they do in a London chop house, which is saying something. Me, I always come prepared.'

With that she unwrapped a cloth which contained a slab of meat and half a loaf of bread. Jemima's mouth watered. Mentally reviewing the few coins in her reticule she decided that it might be best to have a meal now. By the time they reached Bedford it would be well past the time of the evening meal, and she had a nasty idea that Uncle Josh was the sort to have locked up the food until morning, leaving her to go to bed hungry.

The waiting-woman brought her a

plate containing bread, cheese and a pickled onion, which Jemima's friend looked at with scorn. 'That bread looks stale to me, and they've got some nerve selling ordinary rat trap cheese at those prices! It's a scandal, that's what!'

But Jemima was so hungry that she didn't care. She had just eaten the last morsel, mopping up the crumbs with a licked finger, when pandemonium erupted. A large, red-faced woman burst into the room, elbowing her way towards the landlord who was standing behind the bar, wiping out tankards with a grubby towel.

'If you expect me to stay in that room, my man, you're very much mistaken! I've never seen such a dirty hole! Haven't you anything better?'

The landlord shrugged, which infuriated his customer.

'If it was clean it might be a different matter, but that room hasn't seen a duster since Adam was a boy! And as for the bedding, why, that looks like it hasn't been washed after the last person

8

slept there. What I want to know is, what do you intend to do about it?'

The man shrugged again. 'I haven't got no chambermaid, see? The last one, she run off with the dray man, him what's already got a wife up in Leighton Buzzard. There's only me and my daughter to see to everything. Can't be in two places at once, can we? Stands to reason, that.'

A wild idea occurred to Jemima. 'Did you hear what he said? They need a chambermaid here. Do you think they'd hire me?'

Her friend almost choked on a shred of beef. Absentmindedly Jemima patted her on the back. 'Are you moon-crazed, girl? Work in a place like this, with people coming and going all the time? Run off your feet you'd be! And what about your poor auntie, expecting you to come and help her out? Think what your uncle would have to say, his niece living in a common inn!'

'Uncle's never cared tuppence for me before,' Jemima said, with a toss of her head. 'As for my aunt, she'll have to keep the servant she already has. I never did like the idea of that girl being done out of a job because of me.'

'Even so, blood's thicker than water. You get back on that coach the minute they blow the horn, and go to Bedford same as you planned.'

But Jemima had made up her mind. Scrubbing and laundering was something she was used to and she had expected to do that in Bedford, so why not do the same thing here, and get paid for it? Smoothing down her skirts she stood up and made her way to the bar where the landlord was setting up full tankards all in a row.

2

'I heard you say that you're in need of a chambermaid,' Jemima said bravely to the grumpy man.

'Is that so?' He looked her up and down in a way which made her blush, but she stood her ground.

'I'm looking for work, so I'd like the job, if it's still going.'

'Thought you just came in on the stage, missy. You can't tell me you came all the way from London on the off chance there'd be work going here!' He laughed nastily.

'Actually I was on my way to Bedford, but then I heard about the job here so I thought I'd give it a try. Would you hire me, Sir?'

'Might do,' he said, scratching his nose. 'Sixpence a week and all found.'

She took a deep breath. 'A shilling a week!'

'Ninepence, and you'll be on a month's trial. If you're no better than the last silly harlot, you'll be out on your ear and no second chances.'

Jemima nodded. The job was hers!

'My name's Eli Bliss. I'm landlord here. And who might you be?'

'Jemima, Sir, Jemima Coates.'

'Right, then, Jemima. You'll have to cool your heels for a while, this being our busy time, then when the rush dies down our Polly'll show you to your quarters. I'd put you to work this minute only I s'pose you'll need to get your baggage down off the coach and see about getting your money back.' He turned away to attend to a customer.

Jemima went back to her table, her eyes shining. 'I've got the job!'

'Then I only hope you don't live to regret it,' her companion said. 'Look, I'm only going to Meppershall, but if ever you're in trouble you can look me up there. Ask for Bessie Wainwright; anybody will tell you where to find me.'

Jubilantly, Jemima went looking for

the coachman. Some hard bargaining followed as she tried to wrestle the unused portion of her fare from him while he said that the company didn't like him making refunds. Her case was helped when a would-be passenger stepped forward and volunteered to take her place.

The coachman held out his hand for the fare and began grumbling when the man handed the coins to Jemima, saying that was only right. He subsided when she offered to pay him something for delivering a letter to her uncle and promised to wait while she scribbled a few lines.

Bessie nodded in approval when she saw Jemima bent over a sheet of paper, pencil in hand.

'It's lucky you can write,' she remarked. 'Me, I never did get the chance. My parents couldn't afford to send me to school. Still, it never did me any harm, that I will say. 'Education isn't everything,' my old gran used to say. 'Always keep your wits about you, my girl and that's just as good.' Still, your uncle will be glad to get the letter to say you ain't coming. He might worry, else.'

Jemima doubted that, but she didn't want to burn her bridges behind her, so to speak. She might still be glad of a home in Joshua's household in the future. In the meantime she looked forward to seeing a bit of life here at the Angel.

The horrid child had woken up and was now racing about the room, bumping into people's legs and making them spill their drinks. His mother, aware of the angry looks being directed to her, got up and tried to drag him back to her bench, whereupon he went into a screaming tantrum, flinging himself down and drumming his feet on the flagstone floor.

'Just you stop that, my lad, or Boney'll get you!' Bessie snapped and he stopped at once, wide-eyed. 'And mind you behave yourself when we get back on the coach, or you'll feel the

14

weight of my hand!'

Both mother and child glanced at her in awe, and Jemima hid a smile. Perhaps the rest of the journey would be more peaceful than before! Boney of course was Napoleon Bonaparte and England was at war with him. Naughty children were frequently told that if they didn't behave it would be the worse for them, although Jemima thought loyally that there was little prospect of Boney setting foot in England, not with the gallant men of the British army and navy to keep him at bay.

When the horn sounded and her fellow passengers gathered up their belongings and reboarded the stage coach, she watched them leave with mixed feelings. The idea of starting a new life was exciting but at the same time cutting ties with the past was a risk. Still, if things didn't go as she hoped, she wasn't a prisoner at the Angel. She could leave at any time.

'I hear you're joining us, more fool you!' Jemima turned round to find Polly regarding her with an expression of scorn. 'Whatever brought you to the Angle? I'd have thought London would have suited you better than an out of the way spot like this. Catch me staying here if I didn't have to! If Pa let me go I'd be off like a shot. London town, here I come!'

'There was a death in the family,' Jemima murmured. 'All of a sudden the city seemed like a lonely place and I decided to leave. It's different if you live with people belonging to you. I suppose Master Bliss needs you here since this is a family business.'

A sharp 'huh!' was Polly's only reply to that, and she turned on her heel, leaving Jemima to follow. Not surprisingly the room she indicated was an attic at the top of the inn, tucked under a sloping roof. When were servants ever given anything else?

Still, it might have been worse, furnished as it was with a bed, a chair and a rickety table.

While delivering sewing to big houses

Jemima had sometimes met servants who had to sleep in a damp basement, plagued with mice. She shuddered at the thought.

Polly flounced off, without giving any indication of what Jemima was meant to do next. She didn't seem very friendly and that could be a problem because if the pair of them ever had a disagreement the landlord was sure to take sides with his daughter. Jemima was pleasant by nature and usually rubbed along well with everybody, but she had to admit that she hadn't taken much of a liking to Polly.

The girl was a brazen type, wearing a gown that showed far too much bosom and ankle for decency, and Jemima had already noticed that she had a flirtatious manner with the customers that went beyond simple good cheer. Perhaps it was too early to judge?

Possibly the Angel's status as a coaching inn demanded a certain attitude. Just because Polly had a come-hither look in her eye that didn't mean she was bad.

Jemima found her way to the kitchen, where a plump, homely woman was making a number of large apple tarts. She looked up at Jemima's approach.

'You can't come in here, luv! No customers in the kitchen, see?'

'I'm not a customer. I'm the new chambermaid. I didn't know where I was supposed to go, or what I'm meant to do.'

'Oh! Eli hired you, did he? I'm Maggie Tubman, the cook. Leastways, I don't live in, but I might as well, seeing I'm on the spot from dawn to dusk. Eli, he'll tell you what's what when he comes in for his supper. There won't be much doing upstairs once the London coach comes and goes. It won't be long now before that arrives, always supposing there's been no trouble on the road.'

Jemima wanted to ask what Maggie meant by trouble, but at that moment the outer door swung open and a man darted in.

'Give us a cup of tea, will you, Maggie?

Just got time to gulp it down before the coach comes in.' It was the ostler Jemima had spoken to when she first arrived.

'Hello, haven't I seen you somewhere before?' the smile he directed at Jemima almost made her heart turn over.

'I came off the London to Bedford coach,' she murmured. 'We passed each other in the stable yard.'

'Don't tell me you let the coach get away without you! You'll have to spend the night here and go on your way tomorrow.'

'No need for that,' Maggie put in. 'This is Jemima; she's the new chambermaid. And this lad here is Giles. Giles Morton. Don't you take no notice of him. He thinks he knows everything, but really he don't know nothing at all!'

'Aw, Maggie. Fancy telling the poor girl a thing like that. She won't know what to believe now.'

It was evident from their banter that the two were good friends, and this became even more obvious when Giles picked up a lump of pastry and stuffed it into his mouth, with only a token protest from the cook.

'You might at least have put some currants in this for me, Maggie. My old Ma always did that. Nothing like a lump of raw pastry with fruit in it.'

'Huh! Give you worms, that will, eating raw pastry. Don't say I didn't warn you, you great lummox!'

Pleased at the relaxed atmosphere, Jemima added a few teasing words of her own, and soon the room was filled with laughter. She knew she was going to enjoy working here, especially if she managed to spend time with the good-looking Giles. There had been little time for meeting men when she had lived with Aunt Mab but now perhaps things were about to change.

A slight noise caused Jemima to turn around. Polly Bliss was standing in the doorway, one hand on her hip. To judge by the way she was glowering at Jemima she was sending her a message Unmistakably it said, 'hands off! This man is mine!'

3

'Would you like to see the horses?' Jemima had just emptied her pail of water over the cobblestones when Giles sauntered across the yard to her. A glance back at the inn told her that nobody was watching, so she nodded happily.

'Might as well, thanks. I'm finished my work for the moment.'

He led her through the big yard, with its stables doors around the perimeter, into another yard, which looked much the same. Horses of various colours poked their heads over half doors and she was amazed at how many there were.

'Who do all these belong to? Surely not the coach company?'

'Well, of course we always have a few belonging to them, standing ready for when the coachmen want to change horses. Master Bliss owns two or three, some belong to people in the village, and then a lot of customers have their own mounts or teams. This is a livery stable, you know.'

Jemima had been surprised to learn that very few of the Angel's overnight customers were coach passengers, and she said as much to Giles.

'Ah, but then why would they need to stop here, in the middle of nowhere? Unless they arrive late in the day and have to wait for someone to meet them, they'd normally travel on. It's not as if this is a junction point where people change to coaches going in another direction. We do get a lot of folks making their own way, though, and they stop here to give their beasts a rest, and themselves as well, if they're making a long journey. Those are the interesting ones. You never know what to expect from one day to the next.'

'You must like horses, to work in a place like this.'

'I was brought up on a farm. Been

with horses all my life, till I moved to London.'

'But I lived in London, too! How long is it since you were there, Giles?'

But he ignored her question and she wondered why he had changed the subject. Why leave the city where there were many opportunities to work with horses, at a better rate of pay than he'd receive here? Or if he missed country life, why hadn't he returned to the place where he'd grown up? The Angel was neither one thing nor the other.

She sensed a mystery here but decided it was best not to probe at this stage.

'I'd best get back inside. I promised Maggie I'd give her a hand with the vegetables.'

'Funny job for a chambermaid.' Giles grinned.

Jemima shrugged. 'I've nothing better to do with my spare time, and Maggie doesn't have a kitchen maid. It's a crime the way they take advantage of her, but don't tell Master Bliss I said so!'

'Oh, Maggie doesn't care. She likes to keep busy. She's nothing to go home for but a drunken husband, and he spends most of his time in the taproom here. If it wasn't for Maggie they'd be tramping the roads without so much as a roof over their heads. He was a soldier once, old Fred was, and he lost a leg in some battle or other.'

'Yes, I've noticed a man with a peg leg,' Jemima murmured, turning to go indoors.

'Some day when you're not peeling potatoes or shelling peas I'll harness up old Beauty to the dog cart and take you on a tour of the village,' Giles called after her.

Jemima's spirits rose. 'Thanks, I'd love that!'

She very much wanted to get to know Giles better, but the memory of the furious expression in Polly's eyes had stayed with her and before she committed herself she needed to know what there was between the two of them.

'Had a nice walk around the stables, did you?' Maggie's shrewd eyes didn't miss much. 'You want to watch that Giles. Has a way with all the girls, he does. He could charm the birds out of the tree with that smile of his.'

'What about him and Polly, then? Are they betrothed or anything?'

'Bless you, no!' Maggie threw back her head and laughed. 'Oh, I don't doubt she'd like there to be more to it, but it's all one-sided as far as I can make out. He may have squired her round a bit, to the harvest supper and all that, and there may have been kisses exchanged in the moonlight, but that sort of thing doesn't always lead to the altar. No, if you want to try your luck with our Giles, there's nothing to stop you.'

Jemima bent over her bowl of potatoes to hide her blushes. 'Who is that man in the end room?' she asked. 'He surely can't be a traveller, for he's been there ever since I came.' She was wary of the swarthy fellow, having felt the rough edge of his tongue more than once. He had shouted at her when she went to clean his room, telling her to come back later, if she came back at all. She would have been glad to leave the room in the state it was, but she feared Eli's reaction if he found out.

'That's Paul Bell. He's a man as the master does business with,' Maggie replied, tight-lipped.

'What sort of business?'

'Now, you listen to me, my girl! I haven't lived as long as I have without learning that there's some questions it's best not to ask. All right?'

Alarmed by the older woman's tone, Jemima nodded, and got on with her work. In the silence that followed, her mind worked furiously. She could see that Eli Bliss and the dark stranger had something in common; both had an air of suppressed violence and she shivered at the thought of ever running afoul of either man. Still, there was a mystery here, and she wanted to get to the bottom of it.

What business could the pair possibly be involved in? Perhaps Bell was a horse dealer, buying and selling livestock at a profit. Bliss was his partner, who provided stabling for the animals until they were resold. Or, and on this thought her eyes widened, perhaps the animals were stolen and were hidden here until the hue and cry died down. Jemima had heard stories of horses whose coats were dyed another colour so that thieves could avoid detection.

She made up her mind to test this theory by seeking out Giles again. She couldn't ask him outright in case he was part of the scheme, but she could get to know the horses in his care so as to recognise their comings and goings.

'Curiosity killed the cat,' she reminded herself, knowing all the while that she had no intention of letting the matter drop. After all, she needed some sort of excitement to break the monotony of everyday life!

All thoughts of this were driven from her head the next day, when the

Bedford to London coach rolled in. There were no women aboard so the passengers crowded into the bar room where they all demanded service at once.

'I know it's not your job, luv,' Maggie panted, 'but they've got Polly running back and forth with ale, and I can't be in two places at once. Can you take the orders and serve the food to those men, while I dish up in here?'

Jemima was glad to help. Unlike female passengers, who usually required tea and a snack, these men all wanted substantial meals and she was kept busy delivering great plates of meat and potatoes and taking away the dirty dishes before returning with slabs of apple tart and cheese.

Several of the men were reading newspapers while they waited and there was a low rumble of discontent as they commented on what they found printed there. Straining her ears, Jemima caught words here and there such as 'disgusting . . . a scandal . . . something must be done about it before very much longer.'

'What are they all talking about in there?' she demanded, when Giles poked his head round the kitchen door, wanting to know when his dinner was going to be ready.

'Another highway robbery,' he muttered. 'Close to home, too. They held up the stage on the Bedford to Dunstable run. Got away with a fine old haul, too!'

'Now how would you be knowing that?' Maggie demanded, waving a spoon at him, dripping gravy on the kitchen floor. Jemima bent to wipe it up.

'There's a coach and pair out there, just arrived from Ampthill. The coachman told me all about it. It's the talk of the country this morning, and he was all of a dither in case the same highwayman stopped him as well.'

'Was anyone killed?' Maggie wanted to know.

'No, luckily. Apparently he waved a

pistol at the passengers, but they all handed over their valuables without making too much of a fuss, and off he went. It was all over in a few minutes, at least, that's what I was told.'

'I hope that never happens here,' Jemima shivered. 'If someone pointed a pistol at me I think I'd faint right off.'

'Of course it won't happen here, child!' Maggie snapped. 'They find some lonely place to do those hold ups, so they can make their getaway right after. Why would they try their tricks in an inn full of people?'

'I don't know about that.' Giles laughed, winking at Jemima. 'It might come closer to home than you think!'

'You keep your stupid mouth shut!' Maggie roared. 'Don't you know that walls have ears?'

He laughed at that and snatched a triangle of tart from the table, neatly avoiding her threatening spoon.

It was only later, when the inn was quiet again, and Jemima had some time to herself, when a strange thought occurred to her.

That business between the landlord and Paul Bell, could it have something to do with the attacks on the stage-coaches? She chided herself for being fanciful, but the thought refused to go away and she pursued it further.

A lone robber, working out of his own home, would have difficulty hiding from the authorities. Somebody would be sure to wonder how he managed to survive with no visible means of support, and what could he spend his ill-gotten gains on, without drawing attention to himself? Then, too, his horse might be recognised as the one used by the highwayman.

On the other hand, the Angel would be the perfect place to operate from. Strangers were always coming and going, and so were horses. The inn was over three hundred years old and there must be many hiding places within its ancient walls where stolen goods could be stored until it was safe to move them. At a later date a man could board the coach for London, carrying those goods in his ordinary baggage, and once he arrived in the city there was no shortage of places where the items could be sold.

Who, then, could be the highwayman? Polly could be ruled out, being a woman, so that left Eli Bliss, Paul Bell, and perhaps Giles Morton. Eli never seemed to leave the inn, so it probably wasn't him, although she made up her mind to watch him more carefully in future. If she could find out the time of day when the robberies took place that would help her to narrow it down.

Paul Bell? He seemed a more likely prospect, and she would have to keep track of him as well. Reluctantly, she let her mind dwell on Giles. She didn't want it to be him, but he was certainly a suspect. He was good with horses and he had been evasive when she asked why he'd left London. Although it would have been a comfort to confide in him she could well be running into danger, and she knew she must be wary.

4

Jemima had just emerged from what was grandly called the salon when she noticed the man. This was a small withdrawing room where ladies could wait, away from the coarser element of passengers who frequented the bar. The aristocracy travelled in their own private carriages, but many ladies who could not afford such a luxury had to go by public stage coach.

The lady she had just shown into the salon had requested a cup of chocolate and Jemima headed for the kitchen, hoping she'd be offered a snack while the milk was boiling. It was a long time since breakfast!

The man was tall and black-browned and looked vaguely familiar. He was speaking to Polly as if he had a bad smell under his nose, looking her up and down in disdain. Jemima hid a smile, assuming that he was a Methodist who disapproved of the other girl's scanty working garb. But now he stepped aside, barring her way.

'They tell me you're Jemima Coates. I want words with you, missy. Be so kind as to step outside for a moment.'

She opened her eyes wide, wondering what business this unknown traveller might have with her. Eli Bliss looked up, frowning.

'Do as he says, girl, but don't take too long about it! The man says he's your uncle so I suppose you're in no danger from him.'

'But I have a customer, Master Bliss. The lady in the salon wants chocolate.'

'Polly can get it,' he growled. 'Now, get going afore I change my mind.'

Her mind whirling, Jemima followed the man out into the stable yard, where a boy was holding the heads of a team of horses who were hitched to an enormous wagon, piled high with casks and barrels.

'That will do, boy,' Joshua Burnett

muttered, handing over a farthing. The boy snatched the coin and scuttled off.

'I've come to say I'm still prepared to take you into my home,' Joshua said, turning to his niece. 'I must say I was shocked to receive your letter, girl. Such ingratitude I never thought to meet. Your aunt was quite overcome by the thought of it!'

'Probably overcome by the thought she might have to manage alone in a household of fourteen people,' Jemima thought, biting back the furious words.

'I'm sorry to have caused Aunt Dorcas such distress, Uncle,' she said carefully, 'but I like the work here and I understand that she already has a servant girl so I should not be missed.'

'That dunderhead! Half the time she don't know which way is up! Besides, I don't trust servants. Rob you blind, they will, soon as your back is turned. Tis much better to have your own flesh and blood around you. I've told your aunt I'll be bringing you back with me, and she's expecting you, do you see?'

'Yes, Uncle, but as I said, I'm settled here, and well content.'

'I have this load to deliver,' he went on, ignoring her words, 'but I'll stop on the way back and pick you up, is that clear?'

Without waiting for an answer he climbed up to the driver's seat and told the horses to walk on. Well trained, they started off at once. It was clear that Joshua Burnett expected instant obedience from both humans and animals.

Giles walked across the yard, whistling. He winked at Jemima as he passed. She smiled back. She made up her mind that she was certainly not going to Bedford with her uncle. Sorry as she was for poor Aunt Dorcas, that wasn't really her problem. Joshua could hardly carry her off, kicking and screaming.

If there was any possibility of that she would get Eli Bliss on her side. He wouldn't want to lose a good chambermaid, and neither would Polly, who would be forced to do twice the work if Jemima left.

'What did he want?' Eli grunted when Jemima returned, smoothing down her apron as she walked.

'He expects me to go home with him, to help my aunt in the house,' she told him. 'But I'm not going,' she added quickly, as his face darkened with temper. 'I like it here, and I mean to stay.'

'Funny way to treat your own family, girl. You owe the man something, hey?'

She shook her head. 'I haven't even see him since I was four years old, Master Bliss. He's never shown any signs of caring about me before this, and I doubt he cares for me now, except I'd save him the price of a servant's wages. He had no claim on me as long as I lived with my Aunt Mab, but when she died he saw his chance and wrote to tell me to come to Bedford at once. I was on my way there when the coach stopped here.'

'All right, all right, I don't want to

hear your whole life's story,' he scowled. 'If you've nothing better to do than stand here gossiping you can go and scrub out the pantry. Maggie's been on at our Poll to give her a hand, but Poll's got enough to do here.'

Jemima walked away, her face impassive. Polly was leaning against the door frame, her face alight with mischief as she flirted with one of the passengers. Well, let her get on with it. If Jemima was in the kitchen there was more chance of seeing Giles, who was always popping in and out in search of food. She grinned to herself, imagining the look on Eli's face if he ever found out that Giles was gobbling up all the profits.

This gave rise to another thought. How much profit was there to be made in a place like this? Customers paid for rooms and stabling and bought food and drink, but was that enough to keep everyone who worked here? Besides Jemima and Maggie, there was Giles and several stable hands who all had to receive a wage of some sort, yet Eli Bliss seemed quite prosperous.

As part of her duties she had to clean the private rooms where Eli and his daughter lived, and they were filled with the best of everything. The furniture must have cost a pretty penny, and even to Jemima's untrained eye it was evident that the oil paintings on the walls had not been produced by some amateur artist. The carpets which Jemima had to clean with the help of used tea leaves were of the finest quality.

Fires were kept burning in the grates at all times, despite the price of coal, and Polly's wardrobe was bursting with fine gowns in the latest fashion.

'What did that man want with you?' Jemima came to with a start as Giles interrupted her musings. 'A cooper, by the look of him. Too well dressed to be a simple delivery man.'

'That was my uncle Josh, from Bedford.'

'The one you were on your way to

stay with when you got off the stage here.'

'The very same.'

'Nice of him to stop in to see how you're faring,' Maggie murmured, a note of inquiry in her voice.

'He's determined I'm going with him when he comes back this way, and I mean to stay here. I'll get master Bliss to turn him away if I have to.'

'Now that I'd like to see!' Maggie grinned, pausing in her work of cutting up rabbits to put in a pie. 'You'd better put a word in the constable's ear, Giles, in case there's a riot!'

Jemima decided that it might be best if she made herself scarce when her uncle returned. While she didn't want to go with him she had no wish for harm to come to him, either from Eli's great fists, or from the long arm of the law. If anything happened to her husband, what would become of poor Aunt Dorcas, with her great brood of children?

'Can you hide me outside somewhere

40

when Uncle comes back?' she asked Giles, who nodded happily.

'I'd be glad to look after a pretty thing like you! I'll take you up to the hay loft where we can be all alone, that's what I'll do.'

'Now, now, none of that!' Maggie said sharply. 'Don't you listen to him, Jemima Coates! He'll see you out of one sort of trouble and land you in another, and you won't be first, neither, if I knows anything about it!'

Jemima blushed, but Giles laughed easily and planted a smacking kiss on the older woman's cheek. 'You worry too much, Maggie. Now, if I promise not to lay a finger on this young woman, will you find me a wedge of your apple pie? Tis hungry work listening to women's chatter.'

Polly put her head round the door then and glared at Jemima. 'The coach has just come in and you're wanted back there to take orders. And you'd best get out to the yard afore Pa catches you in here, Giles Morton!' She

41

disappeared before either of them could reply.

'Lazy trollop!' Maggie muttered. 'She wouldn't last five minutes in this place if she weren't the daughter of the house. 'You're supposed to be the chambermaid, not the barmaid. You just stand up to her, Jemima, or she'll walk all over you.'

But Jemima knew which side her bread was buttered. She had no doubt that Polly had asserted herself because she'd seen Giles laughing with her rival, which could make her a dangerous enemy. When it came right down to it, Eli would support his daughter in any disagreement between the girls and then Jemima would be out on her ear. In that case she would be forced to go cap in hand to her uncle, where she would no doubt be received with ill grace. She went out in the waiting room and there heard something which made her prick up her ears.

5

The Bedford to London coach had just come in, and Jemima went through to the salon, pushing her way through the throng of men who were eager to quench their thirst at the bar. The elderly lady whom she had previous shown into the salon had come in on a local coach and was waiting for her connection to London. She was hard of hearing and Jemima was afraid that the post horn would go unheard in the inner room, with its thick old walls.

'The coach has arrived, Madam,' she said, smiling. 'It should be ready to leave in about fifteen minutes. Is there anything you'd like in the meantime?'

'Perhaps you'll be kind enough to direct me to the powder room, young woman,' came the reply. 'Be so good as to remain with my luggage until I return. One can trust no-one nowadays!'

Standing in the doorway, keeping an eye on the passenger's hat box and carpet bag, Jemima couldn't help hearing what was being said by the men in the outer room. It was the usual bother about stagecoaches being robbed except that now there was a new twist to the problem

'According to the newspapers there must be a whole gang of these ruffians,' one man announced.

'Or one very busy fellow,' laughed another.

'That hardly seems possible, given the fact that these robberies are now happening all over the shire, and several times a week. A lone highwayman could not possibly be in so many places at once, unless he was riding Pegasus, the winged horse!'

'Blame it on the times we live in, man! The countryside is rife with thieves and beggars. Ship the scoundrels off to fight Boney, that's what I say. Then they'll learn what's what!'

'They have to be caught first!' a third

voice broke in. 'It's my belief that the newspapers have the truth of it. There's a gang at work and some very clever fellow is behind it all. Catch him, and you'll have no more trouble.'

Jemima became aware that Eli Bliss, who usually worked non-stop filling tankards and giving orders to Polly, was standing very still behind the wooden counter. He saw her looking and at once pointed a finger at her while letting out a roar.

'What do you mean by loitering there, girl? Get to work at once unless you want to feel the weight of my hand round your chops!'

Fortunately for Jemima, the old lady had returned to claim her luggage and heard this. 'You'll do nothing of the sort, my man! You should be ashamed of yourself, threatening the poor girl in such a way. She is standing here at my request, as you would know if you'd troubled to ask.'

Eli began bowing and scraping in a way which made Jemima grin, although she was careful not to let him see her expression. He agreed quite meekly when the lady asked if Jemima might carry her bags to the waiting coach, and it seemed that the danger was past for the moment.

So what gave her the notion that Eli had only scolded her in an attempt to create a diversion? Everyone was interested in hearing about the highway robberies, travellers in particular, so there was nothing peculiar about discussing the subject in the Angel. No doubt it was a popular topic of conversation in every tavern and shop in the county.

But it was only when someone had spoken of a possible mastermind behind the problem that he had bawled at her, and why was that? Once again she let her imagination run riot. What if Eli Bliss was a master criminal? All it needed was for some wit to suggest all in jest, that he was ideally suited for the role, with his livery stable in which horses constantly came and went, and the Angel itself, situated in an out of the way location. Eli would laugh it off as a joke, but later, people might think over what had been said, and what might happen then?

Frankly, Jemima didn't care what Eli might be up to, but she was becoming more and more fond of Giles and feared what might happen to him if he was caught up in events.

She made up her mind to get closer to Giles to see what she could find out.

Her chance came two days later. She was busy sweeping out the salon when Polly put her head round the door. 'It's him again, asking to see you.'

'Who is?' Jemima's heart leapt, hoping she was talking about Giles.

'That uncle of yours. Him that's a cooper,' Polly muttered, as if Jemima had numerous uncles, all of whom might turn up at any time. 'He's out in the stable yard. Says he won't come in on account of he don't want to leave the horses.'

On account of he doesn't want to lay

out another farthing to have young Tommy standing with them, Jemima thought, but she hurried outside nevertheless.

'Come along, girl, I don't have all day!' Joshua snapped, preparing to mount to the driver's seat. 'Where's your belongings? You surely have something besides that mop you're waving at me!' Jemima realised she was still clutching the feather duster and felt silly.

'I'm sorry, Uncle, I thought I'd made myself plain. I'm not coming with you, though I thank you for asking. Please give my love to Aunt Dorcas.' She had never met the woman, but thought it wise to speak softly, to avert his wrath.

'You ungrateful wretch!' he snapped. 'Why you choose to stay in this godforsaken place when you could have a good home with me in Bedford is beyond all reason. I've been hearing things about the Angel Inn and it is not the sort of place for a decent young woman like yourself. I'll offer you once last chance, my girl, and if I can't convince you after this then you must go your own way and take the consequences. Don't say I didn't warn you!'

'What sort of things, Uncle?'

'Eh?'

'What sort of things have you heard? Truly, Master Bliss allows no lewd behaviour. Polly and I are well chaperoned by Maggie, who works in the kitchen, and nothing improper ever happens here.'

Joshua Burnett drew himself up to his full height, so red in the face that Jemima feared he might fall down in an apoplectic fit at any moment.

'I meant no such thing, girl, and you should know better than to speak in such a way. It is not fitting that a young woman of your tender years should even know of such matters.'

Jemima thought that the people of Bedford must lead very sheltered lives indeed. Naturally she had never been within miles of a brothel, but nobody could grow up in the poorer parts of London without knowing what went on inside them.

However, there was no point in

upsetting Joshua still more, so she simply asked meekly what he did mean.

'Never you mind,' he said. 'If you insist upon staying here it's best you know nothing.' And with that he climbed into his seat and the wagon left the stable yard.

'I see you're still here, then!' Giles had come up behind Jemima, making her jump.

'Yes, but he gave me a hard time about it. He's really angry, Giles, and I just hope he doesn't go home and take it out on poor Aunt Dorcas.'

'Oh, forget about him! Listen, I've got the day off tomorrow. What about coming out with me? I'll give you that tour of the village I promised.'

'I'd love to, but I don't know what Master Bliss will say.'

'You haven't had a day off since you arrived here, have you? Just leave him to me.'

As they drove away in the trap, Jemima was aware of Polly glowering at them from the doorstep. Giles was busily manoeuvring the vehicle around a large dray which partly blocked their way, and didn't notice. Jemima hoped she wouldn't be made to pay for this outing when she next came into contact with Polly, but she reminded herself that she really was doing nothing wrong. It wasn't her fault if the other girl lusted after a man who wasn't interested. Presumably she had had her chance before Jemima came on the scene but Giles had chosen not to pursue the relationship.

It was pleasant to be bowling along the flowery lanes and Jemima was determined to enjoy this well-earned break from drudgery. Cottage women greeted them while busily shaking the dust from rag rugs and children screamed as they played in the school-yard in a hamlet which the trap passed through. Now and then Jemima caught a glimpse through wide open doors of people working in their homes; Giles told her that these were straw plaiters plying their craft.

'But of course you already know that, if you are Bedfordshire born and bed,' he told her.

'Not really. I was just a toddler when my parents died of cholera and Aunt Mab took me off to London. I don't remember much before that. The only reason I came back here now was that my Uncle Josh offered me a home, and you know how that turned out!'

The conversation dwindled into silence. Jemima felt awkward. She wanted to get to know Giles better but there were only two topics of conversation she could pursue — their daily life at the Angel or questions about his own background, which he seemed reluctant to answer. She couldn't sit there like a stuffed dummy, saying nothing, so she chose to comment on the former.

'Everyone seems upset about the robberies,' she began, choosing her words with care. 'What do you think, Giles? Is there a roving band of highwaymen in the shire? Surely there are too many hold-ups for just one man to be involved.'

'Hard to say.' He shrugged.

'You must have some opinion, Giles!'

'How do I know? Either there's one man working alone, or there's more. That's all there is to it.'

This was highly unsatisfactory and she told him so. 'I've heard the passengers talking about it. Nothing seems to be happening outside of the shire so doesn't that mean that all the robberies in this area have to be connected?'

This observation was met with another shrug and all at once she felt very annoyed with Giles. Her heart told her that she should enjoy the outing, talk lightly of inconsequential things and establish a bond between herself and this man she felt so attracted to.

On the other hand, her inquisitive nature told her to get to the bottom of what was really happening on the roads and a possible connection with the Angel. She took a deep breath.

'I overheard one man say that there must be a very clever man behind all this. Someone who organises the robberies and takes care of the proceeds.'

'Could be.'

'Come on, Giles! Don't you have anything more to say than that?'

'Curiosity killed the cat!' he snapped, turning to look at her through narrowed eyes before returning his gaze to the rutted road ahead.

'And satisfaction brought it back!' she countered. 'I was just thinking that Master Bliss could be such a man. He knows exactly when and where the coaches will be at any give time, and the Angel would be the perfect place for the robbers to report to. Strangers are always coming and going there and nobody thinks anything of that. And there must be a hundred hiding places where stolen goods could be kept until they can be taken to a fence in London.'

'Eli Bliss never leaves the Angel.'

'He might not, but others do! He could pass the goods to a coachman or some passenger who is in his pay, and you know it.'

Giles gave a forced laugh. 'So who is the highwayman, then? Our Polly, or Maggie Tubman?'

'Paul Bell!' she said triumphantly. 'There's something odd about him. Why does he stay in his room for days on end, and where does he go when he does go out? Don't you see, Giles, it all fits very nicely.'

Giles pulled on the reins and the trap shuddered to a halt. 'Now listen here, Jemima! Don't poke your nose into what doesn't concern you, or you'll live to regret it. What may or may not be happening at the Angel is none of your business, and my advice to you is to get on with the work you're paid to do and shut your eyes to everything else.' He clicked his tongue and the horse ambled on again, its head bowed low.

'Then you do know something!' she persisted, but he shook his head.

'All I know is that Paul Bell is a bad man to cross. I wouldn't put it past him to do you a mischief if he found out you were prying into his affairs.'

Jemima shivered. The sun had disappeared and dark clouds were scudding across the sky. 'I expect you're right,' she muttered but they had gone another mile before she realised that Giles hadn't actually denied that something was afoot at the Angel. If he didn't actually know anything then he probably had his suspicions, just as she did. From now on she must keep her ideas to herself. That didn't mean that she would shut her eyes, though! 'It looks like rain, doesn't it? Oughtn't we to start back now?'

'Too late for that!' Giles shouted. 'Here it comes! We'll have to take shelter.'

A derelict barn stood beside the road, and he slid down from the driver's seat and led the horse through the open doorway. Jemima was wearing her best dress, a flimsy muslin, and it was already spotted with wet patches which made the fabric cling to her slender form and she began to shiver with cold.

She deplored the current mode

which made fashionable women delib-erately dampen their gowns so as to display their figures to best advantage. In her opinion they had only themselves to blame if they developed an ague or worse.

By the time she and Giles were seated on some frowsty straw, watching the horse picking unsuccessfully through the pieces in search of food, the rain was pelting down.

'Looks like we'll be here for some time.' Giles sniffed. 'Are you cold, Jemima? Here, you'd better have my jacket. You should have worn something warmer; the weather can change all in a minute at this time of year.'

Jemima accepted gratefully. Wanting to look her best for the outing, she had opted to leave her ratty old shawl behind. This well-worn garment with its moth holes and tattered fringe would have spoiled the appearance of her dress.

This outing was not going as she had hoped. Giles was gloomily watching the teeming rain, probably thinking he'd rather be anywhere but here. How Polly must be gloating! It would be nicer if they were cuddled up together but their relationship hadn't reached that point, and probably never would. Jemima tried to think of something to say to break the silence.

'I suppose we might have some excitement at the Angel this week,' she said at last.

'How do you mean?'

'Oh, something I heard. They're sending constables from London to travel the shire to talk to people. Hoping to find someone who has seen or heard something unusual, I imagine.'

She was shocked by Giles' response to this innocent remark. The colour had drained from his face and he seemed to have difficulty breathing.

'What is it, Giles? What have I said? Is there something wrong? You can tell me, I shan't say anything.'

'You swear?'

'Yes, of course.'

'Then say it!'

'I swear. Cross my heart and hope to die.'

'It's me that'll die if I get found out, Jemima.'

'Surely it can't be as bad as all that,' she told him, thinking 'I knew it! He's one of the highwaymen, working for Eli Bliss!' When he began his tale it was so far from what she had assumed that for a moment she was unable to take it in.

'I'm a deserter from the British navy, Jemima. If they catch me, it's the high jump for me. That's why I can't stay in London, where I'm known, and why I can't go back to my family in the country. Yes, they execute deserters when there's a war on. They have to, or men would be leaving in droves, once they've seen a bit of action.'

'The navy! But why on earth did you sign on in the first place? I could imagine you joining the army, perhaps, where you could look after horses, but whatever possessed you to go to sea?'

'It wasn't my idea,' Giles said bitterly. 'I was working as a groom for a wealthy gentleman in London, hoping to work my way up to being a private coachman some day, when I went to a tavern with friends one night. We had a bit too much to drink and I was rolling home when the press gang caught up with me. Hit me over the head with a cudgel, and the next thing I knew, I woke up aboard ship, being forced to take the King's shilling.'

Jemima gasped. She had heard stories like this while living in London. With the war against Napoleon in full swing, more and more sailors were needed for Nelson's fleet and the only way to make up the numbers was to send out the infamous press gang to round up unwilling victims.

Life in the navy was harsh and cruel at the best of times but even worse in time of war. It was little wonder that few men signed on willingly.

'I was put on a ship that was being outfitted for war,' Giles went on. 'Kept shackled, of course, along with the some other poor devils, so we couldn't escape, but fire broke out on board and we were released to help fight the flames. Or perhaps they didn't want us to burn to death, who knows?

'Anyway, I saw my chance and got away. I was making my way north then I came across the Angel, and like you, I got taken on by Master Bliss. That's my story, Jemima Coates, so what do you think of me now?'

'I'm sure you did the right thing,' she said stoutly. 'Why should you be forced to join the navy if you didn't want to? It's wrong of them to kill people because they don't wish to go to sea. I know they shoot people for cowardice, but it's not as if you deserted in the face of the enemy, is it?'

Giles winced, but said nothing. Jemima looked at his serious face and felt that something else was called for.

'Don't worry, Giles, I'll never breath a word to a living soul. And those constables won't be looking for deserters, will they? They'll have enough on their plates looking for highwaymen! Look, the rain seems to have stopped. Perhaps it's time we started back.'

Giles was quiet throughout the return journey, carefully guiding the horses past the potholes made by the torrential rain. Jemima was silent, too, mulling over what she had just heard. She felt that the revelations had brought her and Giles closer together now. Unless he drew away from her, regretting his shared confidences they had taken a step forward in their relationship. She couldn't wait to find out what would happen next.

6

'You'd better watch out for that Polly!' Maggie warned, as she thumped down her rolling pin on an innocent lump of pastry. 'If looks could kill, you'd have sprouted wings long before now!'

'Oh, I take no notice of her,' Jemima retorted. 'Her nose has been out of joint ever since Giles took me driving the other day. But what's got you all of a tizzy, Maggie? That pastry is going to be tough as old shoe leather by the time you've done with it. It's not like you to be so heavy handed.'

'Ay, I always did have a light hand with pastry,' Maggie admitted, 'but today I'm upset, right enough.' She lowered her voice. 'It's them constables or whatever they call themselves, come from London. Poking and prying into every nook and corner, they are. Why, one of them even took a stick and started stirring it into my floor barrel! You can stop that at once, my man, I told him, or that flour won't be fit to feed to man or beast!

'I'm only doing my duty, Madam,' he says. 'We're searching for this here highwayman what's been terrorising the shire.'

'Well, says I, you won't find him in there, and you stop that at once or you'll get a thick ear!'

'Where are they now?' Jemima asked, wondering if she should slip out to warn Giles.

'Gone upstairs. Hunting through the guest chambers and leaving everything in a great mess, I shouldn't wonder. They're not just looking for strangers, of course. They want clues as well.'

Jemima sped up the worn stairs, hoping to see what they were up to. Let Maggie think she was being a conscientious chambermaid, making sure that the constables left everything in order. What she really wanted was to see if they had got into Paul Bell's room.

Bell wasn't there, and neither were the constables. She could hear them moving about on the floor above, where the servants' quarters were. Not that many of the rooms were used, because Polly slept in the private family wing and Giles and the other men slept over the stables.

The door to Bell's room stood ajar, and she peeped inside, her heart thumping. There was little to see. The bed was unmade, although whether Bell had left it that way or the men had pulled it apart she couldn't say. The stub of a candle in a china candlestick was the only item on the bedside table, which was covered with a film of dust, and a grubby shirt carelessly over the back of a chair as if its owner had undressed in a hurry.

A huge press on the far wall had been left with its door gaping open but that was empty. Either Bell had gone for good, taking his things with him, or he used this room as temporary accommodation only, making his real home elsewhere. Jemima would have given a lot to know where that might be.

The two constables came clattering down the stairs, stopping when she appeared in the doorway.

'Hey, you! What are you about, then? Sneaking around in that man's room?'

Jemima drew herself up. 'I was not sneaking, as you call it,' she snapped. 'I'm the chambermaid here. It's my job to keep these rooms clean and tidy, and if you've made a mess I'll have to clear it up, or I'll be in trouble with the master.'

'Then perhaps you can tell us about the man who stays in this room?'

She shrugged. 'Guests come and go. They're never here long enough for me to get to know them, even if I wanted to.'

The taller of the two men looked at her with narrowed eyes. 'Ah, but the man who has this room isn't your common or garden traveller, is he? I've heard that he stays here permanent, like. So what can you tell us about him?'

'I know nothing about him. I've never even been in this room before today. The master doesn't like us to meddle in the customers' business.' It was the wrong thing to say.

'Is that so! Well, this is a queer place to be sure! In any inn where I've ever been they attend to the rooms, and to the guests' wants, too. So our friend keeps himself to himself, does he? Likes to pay extra for a chamber all to himself, when lesser men sleep four to a room. Must be a wealthy sort of fellow! What does he do for a living then?'

'I have no idea. Perhaps he has private means.' It crossed Jemima's mind to say that Bell was in business with Eli Bliss, but something warned her to keep quiet about that. Let Bliss explain it if he could.

The constable guffawed. 'A gentleman, is he? Funny sort of gentleman if he chooses to live in a place like this, eh?'

Jemima shrugged. 'As I say, I know nothing about him. Now, will you please let me go about my work? I need this job and you'll get me dismissed if I fall behind.'

Reluctantly they let her go. She felt rather proud of her part in this useless exchange. If they fastened on Paul Bell as a likely suspect they would waste little time on Giles, and that was all to the good.

Much later, when the two men had mounted their horses and ridden away, she went looking for Giles, on the pretext of carrying a message to him from one of the guests whose horse was resting in the stable. This yarn was for Polly's benefit. Jemima didn't want her to follow and overhear something she shouldn't.

She found Giles in one of the stalls, busily currying a tall black mare. He was whistling softly between his teeth and the animal stood quietly, showing no concern when Jemima approached.

'Have they gone?' she began, although she had already seen them leave. She wanted to approach the subject in a roundabout way, in case any of Giles' work mates were within earshot.

'Ay, and good riddance. They were in here for an hour or more, pestering us with questions.'

'Did they say anything about you-know-what?'

He shot her a warning look. 'They mostly wanted to know about the horses we have standing at livery. Who owns them. How long they've been here, and why. They made notes of everything.'

She managed a little laugh. 'So they don't suspect that you or one of the boys might be this highwayman they're looking for, then.'

'Oh, they asked enough questions! How long had we been working here, where we come from, all that. Wanted to know why I'd left London, where I got good money working for a gentle-man who kept his own carriage. I told them I'm a country chap. Couldn't stand all the smoke and dirt. They wanted to know how I heard about the

Angel. I took a leaf out of your book and said I was on my way to Bedford to see an uncle, when the stage stopped here and I hopped off!'

Jemima was aghast. 'But what if they check out your story, Giles?'

'Don't see how they can. They never asked the name of my uncle, or my master in London. I tried to act a bit simple while I was at it. I could see they were sneering at me, thinking I'd never have the wit to hold up a stage coach and get away with it.'

There was a scuffing sound outside, and Jemima pointed wordlessly to the half door to warn Giles. Somebody had been lurking there, but how much had they heard?

Jemima raised her finger to her lips and pointed towards the door.

'There's nobody there,' Giles told her, not pausing in his work. 'It's just the wind rattling the door.'

Exasperated, she flung the door open to reveal Polly, who straightened up and flounced inside, looking defiant.

'I might have known it would be you,' Jemima sniffed. 'Butting in where you're not wanted!'

'I could say the same about you!' came the retort. 'Everything in the garden was lovely until you came on the scene, trying to take my sweetheart away from me!'

'Huh! What sweetheart is that, then?' The two girls stared at each other like two cats spoiling for a fight.

'You've got one already,' Polly snapped. 'I don't know why I bother with you, you faithless brute. I thought we was to be wed, but now you never give me the time of day, since this one arrived. Well, I know what to do about that! I've only to snap my fingers and Pa will see to the pair of you. You'll get the horsewhipping you deserve, Giles Morton, and this drab will find herself out on the road before she knows which way is up!'

'You know we never said nothing about getting wed,' Giles grunted. 'Oh, I'll allow as there was a bit of kissing and hugging, but it was all in good part.

71

It takes more than that to make a marriage, Polly Bliss, a lot more.'

'You can tell her that, an' all!' Polly said bitterly, jabbing an insistent finger in Jemima's face, making her take a step back.

'No need to, then. She means nothing to me, Poll.'

That hurt. If Jemima was honest she had to admit to herself that there was no understanding between Giles and herself, not even a kiss. All their relationship amounted to was a lot of chit chat when they met, and that one outing into the countryside.

Still, she believed that in sharing his secret with her it had put them on a different footing, for didn't that prove that he trusted her with his life? Surely that meant something?

'Well?' Polly demanded, 'do I go to Pa, or not?'

'You can please yourself as far as I'm concerned,' Giles answered taking up the dandy brush and resuming work on the horse. 'But don't take it out on

Jemima. She's done nothing to be ashamed of.'

'That's as may be, but what'll happen to you if I tell Pa what I know?'

'And what might that be?'

'Why, what I just heard the two of you talking about, of course.'

Jemima sucked in her breath, wondering how much the other girl had heard. It all depended on how long she had been standing there with her ear pressed to the crack. She was sure that nothing had been said about Giles being a deserter from the navy, but a listener could easily have gathered that he had something to hide.

'I suppose you're thinking that Giles is the highwayman everyone is looking for,' she said now. 'Well, you're wrong, Polly. The constables have spoken to him, same as everybody else who works here, and they've gone on their way satisfied he's not involved.'

Polly threw back her head and laughed long and hard. 'Oh, I don't think that,' she gasped, 'not at all. I wouldn't, you see, not when I know what's really going on!'

They stared at her in astonishment. 'Oh yes,' she went on, 'it's been happening right under your noses all the time, only you're too stupid to see it. Or maybe Pa is too sharp for you. He's a clever man, is my Pa. Even the police and the justices haven't working it out because, you see, there isn't just one highwayman at work, there's a whole team of them, scattered around the shire.

'They've barely got going yet, but the plan is to step up the business so it confuses the authorities. They'll rush up to Bedford or Dunstable when trouble breaks out there, and then they'll have to scurry to some other place far away when there's another hold up.'

She stopped, looking triumphant. Jemima sat down on an upturned pail, feeling weak at the knees. Giles slapped the mare on the rump and stepped out of the stall, carefully putting the bar in place behind him.

'I don't believe you, Poll. If this was true, you'd never dare to spill the beans. Your Pa would tan the hide off you. What's to stop us turning informer now, then?'

'Cos Pa would shoot the pair of you before you could get very far. D'you think he'd let you spoil everything he's worked so hard for?'

Jemima felt sick. They were in grave danger, she was sure. Polly had only to go to Eli Bliss and spin some tale about how they had uncovered his plot, and he might do away with both of them, even if they had no intention of going to the authorities. He could never take that chance. She gulped, searching for the right words.

'I don't believe you either, Polly. This is just your way of getting attention. Why, if the master knew you were saying things like this you'd be in big trouble. He'd do anything to avoid getting caught, knowing he'd swing for doing this. It wouldn't be just Giles and me he'd kill. You'd be for it too, daughter or no daughter.'

She paused, to see what effect her words might be having. She was pleased to see that Polly's face had turned a pasty grey.

'It was just a joke,' she muttered, her voice so low that Jemima had to strain to hear her. 'Course I wouldn't say nothing if it was true; what d'you take me for?'

'Then you'd better shut up in future,' Giles advised. 'True or no, your Pa wouldn't like to hear you talking like that, and what if someone else heard you? They'd haul him in front of the justices, and who knows what would happen then?'

Polly nodded sullenly. 'All the same, I know you've got something to hide, Giles Morton, and I'm going to find out what it is. Unless you stay away from this one' — and here she jerked a thumb at Jemima — 'I'll go straight to Pa and tell him what I know.'

'That makes two of us,' Giles assured her, and she turned to Jemima and ordered her to get back to the house and get on with her work. Jemima did as she was told, not because she let Polly tell her what to do, but because she needed to think. As she stumbled across the cobbles she looked back once and saw that Polly was now hanging over the half door, laughing and flirting with Giles as if the previous exchange had never taken place.

'Where did you get to?' Maggie wanted to know, when Jemima slipped into the kitchen, hoping she hadn't been missed.

'Just went to see Giles.'

'I thought as much! Sweet on him, ain't yer?'

Jemima hung her head. 'Is there anything wrong with that?'

'No, there is not, although in my experience all men are tarred with the same brush and we poor weak women would be better off avoiding them altogether. Still, if we all thought that way the human race would come to an end, eh? So why have you come back

77

looking like you lost a threepenny bit and found a farthing?'

'Polly.'

'Ah! Followed you there, did she, and caught you having a bit of a kiss and a cuddle, mebbe? I warned you to watch out for her, Jemima Coates. A right jealous biddy she be, and no mistake.'

Jemima longed to confide in Maggie, but she didn't dare. She had to keep Giles' secret, of course, and neither could she talk about what Polly had said. Maggie probably knew more about what went on at the Angel than anyone else, having been here such a long time.

'Did those officers of the law have a word with you, girl?'

'Yes, Maggie. They kept asking me about Paul Bell. Where was he from. Where is he now. What sort of business does he engage in. that sort of thing.'

'And what did you say to that?' Maggie asked, starting to chop carrots with a wicked looking knife.

'What could I say? I don't know anything about him. I thought of saying that he's in business with the master, then I thought I'd better not, so I just told them I didn't know, and they seemed to accept that.'

'And just you keep saying that, if you're asked again. You were right to say nothing; Master Bliss wouldn't like it. Them as wants to stay on the right side of him keeps their opinions to themselves, do you understand?'

'That doesn't stop us thinking, though, does it?' Jemima asked, throwing caution to the winds. 'I'd never say a word outside this room, but I have wondered if mister Bell is the highwayman they're all talking about. It's true what the officers said, Maggie. If he's a gentleman with private means, what's he doing in a place like this?'

'A gentleman! Huh, that's rich!'

'So what do you think, then? Who is he really?'

'I don't know and I don't care. All I can say is that a highwayman he is not, and I've already said far too much, so don't ask me any more questions!'

7

Life returned to normal with the departure of the police investigators. There was still no sign of Paul Bell, but Eli Bliss continued as the somewhat morose host of the Angel, while Polly flounced around with her nose in the air, ignoring her rival.

As for Jemima, she thought it best to stay away from Giles for the time being. She told herself that it was to keep Polly sweet, but underneath it all she was hurt by his insistence that she meant nothing to him. She had to admit that he had never indicated otherwise, yet did he have to be so definite about it? She realised that she was falling in love with him, and it upset her that the possibility of any future relationship seemed doomed.

'Where's that Polly?' Maggie grumbled. 'She's never about when she's wanted.

She can think herself lucky she's the daughter of the house instead of a paid servant or she wouldn't last two minutes round here!' This was her usual cry.

'Can I help?' Jemima asked, having nothing better to do at the moment.

'You can save my poor old legs by taking that tray to the master,' Maggie told her, wiping her brow with the back of her hand. 'I've got all these tarts to get ready for tomorrow, and what does he do? Says he wants a bowl of broth and a meat pie in his room, and supper over not an hour since. Mind and not fill the bowl too full, in case it slops over on the way. Very particular about his food, is Master Bliss, and likely to throw the tray at your head if he don't like what he sees.'

That Jemima could well believe, for she had seen him in a temper before, although thankfully not with her.

'And he'll want a clean napkin, too,' Maggie went on. 'He's not a man as likes food spilled down his front, for all he looks so untidy most of the time.'

As Jemima approached Eli's private apartments, she heard the sound of voices inside: Polly, sounding shrill, and her father's bass tones. She knocked timidly, wanting to make them aware of her presence. She would have given a lot to know what they were saying, but judged it wise to give Polly no chance to accuse her of snooping after the other girl's previous comments.

'Put it down there and get out!' Eli snapped, and Jemima sketched a curtsey and left, gently closing the door behind her. Pausing, she could just make out what they were saying.

'I haven't had a new gown for months, Pa!'

'You've a press full of gowns, girl.'

'All out of fashion. If you want me to attract the customers I have to look the part.'

'Then get the pedlar to sell you a bale of poplin. It's about time you learned to sew, or maybe that Jemima can help you. She used to earn her living by it up London.'

Polly made a rude noise with her lips and Jemima grinned. She no more wanted to make a dress for the landlord's daughter than Polly wanted her to be involved.

'You must think I'm made of money,' Eli grunted, a statement which drew a loud laugh from Polly.

'Well, aren't you, Pa?'

'Maybe I am, maybe I ain't, but the less said about that the better. You never know who might hear you.'

'Please, Pa,' Polly wheedled. 'I want to see what ladies of fashion are wearing now. That's why I don't want nothing homemade. Stuck out here in the middle of nowhere I don't know what's going on in the outside world. It's ages since I had a few days away from home. Why can't I go up London and have a look around?'

There was a long silence as Eli apparently pondered this remark, and just when Jemima was about to give up and tiptoe away, he began to speak.

'You going away might not be a bad idea, so long as you let it be known you've shopping to do. You can take the morning coach if there's room.'

There was the sound of Polly clapping her hands in glee, following by a disappointed sigh when he went on to say that she wasn't jaunting off to London, but travelling in quite the other direction.

'I want you to carry a message to Dunstable. I can't trust the coachman. When you've delivered it you can go shopping. You're sure to find something to your liking there, but not at London prices.'

Polly murmured something that Jemima couldn't catch, and her father countered with something that sounded like well. She frowned. What was he talking about? Hell, smell, dell? No, it must be Bell, of course. The mystery guest had not yet returned. Was he waiting for a sign from the landlord that it was now safe to return?

The sound of footsteps echoed down the passage and she made a hasty retreat, flying up the stairs to her room. She pushed the door open and almost jumped out of her skin when she saw Giles sprawled in the bedside chair.

'What are you doing here?' she gasped, quite unnerved by the encounter.

'Haven't seen you around lately,' he said cheekily. 'I thought you must have died and gone to heaven, so I came to find out.'

'Not that you care!' Jemima tossed her head, although inside she was overjoyed to see him.

'What's that supposed to mean?'

'Well, after what you told Polly I got the idea that I mean less to you than one of your horses.'

'Oh, take no notice of that. I had to say something to put her off the scent, didn't I?'

He stood up and planted a hearty kiss on her unresisting mouth.

'Here, that's enough of that!' Jemima

told him, as she pushed him away. 'You can't come into a decent girl's bedroom and try to take advantage. If you want to spend time with me you can meet me outside. What if Polly came along and caught us together? You know what would happen then.'

'Oh, her! You can't tell me she ever comes up to the servants' quarters when she lives in comfort downstairs.'

'Not unless she comes up to Paul Bell's room for some reason. It's directly below this one, in case you haven't noticed.'

'Why would she want to do that? He's gone, as far as I know.'

'For the moment, but I think she's supposed to carry a message to him tomorrow, and I don't know if that's just by word of mouth, or something more. He might have something hidden in his room that the master wants her to deliver to him.'

Giles listened carefully as Jemima told him what she had overheard. Then he whistled softly. 'Dunstable, eh! I wonder what that means?'

'Isn't it obvious? He's one of the highwaymen in Eli's pay but he had to go into hiding when the investigators came. Now Polly is supposed to let him know it's safe to return.'

'I don't know why he'd go all the way to Dunstable to hide out when there are plenty of places closer to home. The Angel is a very old building. I've heard rumours that there are secret hiding places somewhere inside these walls, dating from the days when priests were forbidden to say the Mass on pain of death. Surely Bill would hole up there until the coast was clear. Are you sure it was him they were talking about?'

Jemima had to admit that it might not be.

'Speaking of hiding places,' Giles went on, his eyes sparkling, 'now's our chance to explore his room to see what we can find.'

'I've already been in there, Giles, and there's absolutely nothing to see.'

'Not on the surface, perhaps, but

there may be some sliding panel or hidden trapdoor. It's worth a try, anyway.'

Shaking with nerves, Jemima kept watch at the foot of the stairs, praying that nobody would come along and catch them in the act. After what seemed an eternity Giles came down, shaking his head.

'Not a thing! I thought he'd have money hidden away at the very least.'

'I told you so!' Jemima muttered, still trembling after her long wait. 'Now, will you get back where you belong before somebody sees you?'

'Not before we've said a proper goodbye,' he grinned, taking her in his arms and placing a lingering kiss on her lips. She felt herself responding gladly. Then he was gone, leaving her shivering for quite another reason.

The next day the dust-covered coach from London trundled in and there was the usual commotion as the passengers disembarked, demanding food and drink. Polly duly boarded when it was ready to leave again, after boasting to everyone within earshot that her loving father was treating her to a new wardrobe.

Jemima watched her go, feeling thoughtful. She remembered what Maggie had hinted about Paul Bell being something quite different from a highwayman and she would have given a lot to know just what the older woman had meant by that remark. Perhaps it was something quite simple; when Jemima had first come to the Angel she had suspected the men of being part of a ring of horse thieves and that was still possible. Now that she trusted Giles she must ask him about that.

Meanwhile she must get on with her work, which was heavier than usual because she now had Polly's duties to perform as well as her own.

The following morning the Bedford to London stage coach was late in arriving. The waiting room was silent and even Eli Bliss seemed worried and restless. For once there were no overnight guests at the Angel, and the rooms stood ready for occupancy, in case there were new customers from one of the day's incoming coaches.

'Nothing doing in the yard?' Maggie asked, when Giles and the other outside workers wandered into her kitchen in search of a 'stay bit' to tide them over until the noon meal.

'Everything's ship shape for now,' Giles replied. 'No travellers at the moment, just the regulars to look after.' He meant the horses, of course, those who normally stood at livery in the inner yard.

'Funny the stage is late,' one of the other lads remarked, as he crammed bread and cheese into his mouth. 'Mebbe a wheel come off or summat.'

'Don't speak with your mouth full,' Maggie admonished, raising her eyebrows at the unlovely sight of the lad chewing with his mouth open. 'And must you choke down so much all at once?'

He responded by pushing another

crust into his gaping maw. 'If you was a poor orphan like me you'd know to grab it while you can, missus.'

This exchange was interrupted by the sound of a vehicle pulling up outside.

'That's the coach now, lads. Out you go!' Maggie removed a tray of tarts out of the reach of the poor orphan, laughing as she did so. 'And go on, Jemima, you'll be wanted out there to help serve ale.'

As soon as the passengers poured inside Jemima realised that this was not the usual crowd of folks yawning and stretching, asking about food, and rooms for the night, or where the privy was to be found. They were silent and shocked and one woman was openly weeping. They stood in a huddle as if bewildered, like sheep that have been herded into a pen by a snappy sheepdog.

'Whatever is the matter?' she asked, as she steered the tearful woman towards a bench where she could sit down.

'We were held up on the road,' the woman whispered. 'Oh, dreadful it was! A masked man, all dressed in black, brandishing a pistol. He told us to give him our valuables or somebody would get killed. He took everything I had in my reticule, all my money and then he made me hand over my mother's brooch that was left to me when she died. It was only made of tin and not worth much, except that I treasured it because it belonged to her. I don't know why he had to take that. He won't get much for it if he tries to sell it.'

'What was it like, your brooch?' Jemima asked, not knowing what else to say to comfort the poor soul but thinking that perhaps it would help her to talk about it.

'It was blue, like a cornflower. Her favourite flower, that was. My dad gave it to her when they was courting. It's all I had left of them now they're dead, and now that's gone too!'

The tears began to flood again, and a tide of fury welled up in Jemima to think that anyone could be so cruel as to deprive a woman of a cheap little piece of jewellery when it could be worth nothing to him.

'Would you like a cup of tea?' she asked, realising as she spoke that all the money the woman possessed had been take from her. 'It's all right; it'll be on the house.'

Receiving a grateful nod in return she pushed her way through the throng to get to the kitchen. She wouldn't put it past Eli Bliss to refuse to serve customers who had been made penniless by the hold-up but she didn't care. If necessary she would pay for the tea out of her own pocket.

'You'll do nothing of the sort!' Maggie told her. 'If the master kicks up a fuss, you just leave him to me. I warrant he won't be refusing to serve ale to the men, cash down or not. Likes to play the big man, he does! Well, I can play the big woman!'

Jemima was amused by this, because Maggie took frequent tastes of the food she was cooking to make sure it was properly flavoured, and as a result she was well padded.

'You can slip her a bit of seed cake while you're at it,' the cook went on. 'Nothing like a strong cup of tea and a bit of seed cake when you want bucking up!'

Jemima was turning away after serving the woman when she caught sight of Giles, signalling wildly from the door. Not wanting anyone to notice what was happening she went to his side as quickly as possible.

'He's back!' Giles hissed. 'Paul Bell. Rode into the yard not five minutes since. The horse has been ridden hard. I reckon they've come far and fast. The poor beast was foaming at the mouth and sweating. I've told young Jem to walk him about until he cools down, or it'll founder, sure enough.'

'Him,' you say. 'It's not a mare then. What colour is it?'

Giles looked puzzled. 'It's a bay, a bay gelding. What about it? What does

94

it matter what sort the animal is? That fool has almost run it into the ground, and that's all that matters to me.'

'Never mind. I'll tell you later.' Jemima went back to the female passenger and stood with her hand on one hip, hoping that Eli, if he noticed, would think she was taking an order.

'What colour was the highwayman's horse?' she demanded.

'Black, it was. A big black horse, and the man was dressed all in black, too. He looked like a devil straight out of hell. I remember thinking that at the time, especially after I heard the shot. Why did you want to know?'

'I just wondered,' Jemima improvised. 'I'm afraid he might come here and I want to be on the look out for a stranger on a horse of that colour.'

It was a feeble enough excuse, but the woman nodded in agreement. 'You're probably safe enough, dearie. These villains waylay innocent people on the high road because they can make a quick getaway when they've done

95

their evil work. In a place like this there are likely to be too many men about who could fight back, perhaps armed with sabres or muskets for all we know. Such as they would never come to the Angel, you may count on it.'

'But perhaps they already have,' Jemima mused, knowing that Bell had returned as mysteriously as he had left. True, he had ridden in on a bay gelding and this coach had been robbed by a man on a black horse, but what did that signify? If he had associates all over the countryside it would have been easy to change horses after doing the deed.

A stout, well-dressed passenger grabbed at her as she made her way back to the kitchen. 'A meat pie, girl, and be quick about it!' he ordered. Annoyed, she pulled her skirts from his grasp and stared him down.

'Have you money to pay for it, sir?' she asked, in a tone bordering on insolence. If Eli heard and reprimanded her she would insist that she wasn't there to be manhandled by rude customers, but the customer noticed nothing wrong.

'I certainly do! With so much trouble on the roads these days a wise man will carry two purses, one to hand over to the thieves and the other hidden well away!' He produced a fat leather pouch and she nodded and hurried away. When she returned he was deep in conversation with another man, and what she heard interested her very much.

'You perhaps saw nothing, Sir, for you were seated inside,' the newcomer began. 'I was riding on the outside, and I could see that among the baggage there was a small brass-bound trunk. That shot you heard was the villain shooting off the padlock, and he forced me to transfer what was inside to his saddlebags, on the threat of being shot myself!' He paused dramatically to let this information sink in.

'What was in those bags? You may well ask! Coin of the realm, my dear sir, golden guineas to judge by the rattle they made as I passed the bags over.

The coachman later told me that they were being sent to Barclay's Bank in London, for what purpose he could not tell. He thought it strange that the owners, whoever they are, took the risk of sending such a valuable cargo on a public conveyance without a man to guard it.'

'Then the highwayman must have had prior knowledge that the money was to be on the coach that day, or why go to the chest so directly? There is more to this than meets the eye.'

Jemima agreed. Having handed over the pie and received payment she hastened back to the kitchen, passing straight through it and out into the stable yard.

'Giles! Did you unsaddle Paul Bell's horse yourself? Did you get a look at his saddlebags at all?'

'Not a chance. He unbuckled them himself and took them into the inn.'

'Did they seem heavy to you?'

'Can't say as I really noticed. I had too much else to take care of, with everyone stumbling out of the coach, bemoaning their losses. He rushed inside without a thought for the horse, leaving the poor devil standing there, heaving.'

'There was a chest of money on board, and apparently the highwayman went straight for it. People seem to think he knew it was there.'

'And Eli Bliss sent our Polly off to Dunstable with a message for some-body! What if he knew that this money was to be aboard the coach today? Did he send word to his associates to go out and pick it up? Or, as we first thought, was he only letting Bell know it was safe to return?'

'Unless Paul Bell and the highway-man are one and the same,' Jemima replied, 'and that's what I believe.'

8

Polly returned from her jaunt, but how different she looked from the dowdy, rather grubby young woman who had left the Angel several days earlier. She tripped off the coach followed by the admiring glances of several male passengers who were quite obviously entranced by her.

She wore a floaty pink dress, the skirts of which billowed as she moved, and satin shoes which were much too dainty to survive a walk in the rain, or so Jemima thought as she looked at this vision of beauty. Her straw bonnet, which in shape resembled a coal scuttle, was decorated with a rosette of different coloured ribbons, designed so this headgear could be worn with a variety of outfits.

The crowning glory of Polly's new image was a cloak resembling those worn by British army officers, a garment all the rage among fashionable ladies. Ordinary women wore shawls, both indoors and out, as befitted their less exalted station in life.

Jemima had never possessed such garments, yet she could certainly admire them on someone else, and despite her dislike of the other girl she was able to feel pleased for her. After all, Polly didn't have much of a life, stuck here at the Angel with her difficult father. She deserved something nice to happen to her once in a while. Sadly, this saintly feeling didn't last long.

'Here, you take this!' Polly snapped, holding out her travelling bag in Jemima's direction.

'What am I supposed to do with it?' Jemima demanded, assuming that the bag held Polly's everyday clothes. Surely she wasn't suggesting that Jemima should wear her castoffs?

'Wash my things, of course,' the other girl ordered. 'There's mud all round the hem of my dress and I don't want it to sink in. You'd better let it soak for a while and then give it a good rubbing.'

Jemima's jaw dropped. 'I'll have you know I work here as a chambermaid, Polly Bliss, not a washerwoman! I'm not your servant, either, even if you have come home dressed up like a dog's dinner!'

'I'll make you pay for that, you see if I don't!' Polly spoke sweetly, well aware that the eye of her admirers were still on her, but the cold glare she focused on the other girl made Jemima shiver. Not trusting herself to answer back calmly she walked off to the kitchen with as much dignity as she could muster.

'What's the matter with you?' Maggie wanted to know. 'You've a look on your face that would sour the milk!'

'It's that Polly!' Jemima said, through gritted teeth.

'Oh, she's back then, is she?'

'She is that, and dressed in new clothes from head to foot. What she has on must have cost her father a pretty penny.'

'I dare say.' Maggie spoke mildly for her. 'It's a poor lookout if a man can't treat his only daughter to a new gown now and then. If your own poor father was still alive he'd doubtless do the same for you.'

'I'm not jealous, if that's what you're thinking, Maggie. It's just the way she tried to lord it over me, telling me to wash her dirty clothes, if you please!'

'Take no notice, girl. I expect she was just trying to impress the folk she travelled with on the coach. I know just what's the matter with your Polly; she's trying to attract a husband to take her away from all this, and who can blame her? Not that marriage does much good for a woman, or that's been my experience, at least, but we all need a bit of romance in our lives, or what were we put here on earth for?'

Jemima had no doubt that the romance Polly was hoping for had something to do with Giles Morton, and so it proved to be. Late that evening Jemima was in the kitchen, trying to make up a tray for an elderly woman who was staying in one of the guest rooms. She was cursing under her breath because Maggie had long since gone home and had left almost everything locked up and Jemima had been forced to go to Eli Bliss to borrow his master keys.

When the lady had been asked earlier if there was anything she needed she had said no, only to ring imperiously after everyone had gone to bed, demanding chocolate and something to eat. Between the scolding she had received from Eli, who was furious at being disturbed, and the guest's sharp tongue, Jemima had just about had enough of working at the Angel.

The outer door flew open and Polly stood on the threshold, her bosom heaving. She was still wearing her finery but her hair was hanging down her back in disarray instead of in the fashionable style she had worn earlier, much like the ears on a spaniel.

'I hate you, Jemima Coates!' she shouted. 'I'll never forgive you for this, never!' She stormed across the room and sailed through the inner door, slamming it behind her. Jemima closed the yard door, longing to scream.

'No prizes for guessing what she's been up to!' she told herself, as she balanced the candlestick on a corner of the tray and went upstairs. By the time she had dealt with the woman's further demands — despite the fact that it was summer the room was too cold and the fire needed making up — she was too tired to sleep. On an impulse she threw on her shawl and went across to the stable block, thankful for the moon which lit her way.

She found Giles perched on a stool, looking up at the sky. He started when he realised that he wasn't alone.

'This seems to be my night for receiving fair maidens,' he drawled. 'First our Polly and now the fair Jemima. To what do I owe the pleasure?'

'This isn't funny, Giles! I've just had Polly bawling at me in the kitchen, telling me she hates me, and I want to know what that was all about!'

'Can't you guess? She came out here and all but threw herself at me, and when I told her I wasn't interested, she got upset.'

'Couldn't you have been a bit more tactful? Nobody likes to be rejected.'

'I did. I was!' Giles sounded aggrieved. 'I even told her she looks lovely in that new rig-out. Then she went on and on about how she's loved me since the first day she set eyes on me, that sort of rot, and I said I was sorry, that I was in love with you.'

Jemima's heart began to thud. 'Really? I mean, were you just saying that to get rid of her, or are you really in love with me?'

Giles grinned. 'Wouldn't you like to know!'

Incensed, she began pounding on his chest with both fists. Why were men always so infuriating? Grasping her by both wrists he drew her towards him and his lips found hers. After a long kiss which left her breathless he looked at her tenderly and laughed softly.

'There, does that tell you wanted to know?'

It didn't, of course. She would have preferred a solemn declaration of his everlasting love for her, but it was a good start. Standing in the moonlight, wrapped around by a soft summer breeze, she wished that the night would never end.

Intent upon each other, neither Jemima nor Giles were aware of a white face looking down on them from an upper window. Polly had gone up to Jemima's room to make sure that she was safely in bed and nowhere near Giles, and she could see by the light of the moon that her fears had come true. She vowed to hurt both of them, not yet knowing that the perfect opportunity would arise the very next day.

The London coach pulled in, followed by two men on horseback.

Dismounting stiffly, one of them greeted Giles like an old acquaintance, as indeed he was.

'Well, I'll be a monkey's uncle! You're the last person I expected to see here!'

'Barney Molloy!' Giles responded, without enthusiasm. 'Keep your voice down, can't you? I don't want the whole world knowing my business!'

'Don't say you're too proud to acknowledge an old mate, man! Come on inside and we'll have a jar together for old time's sake.'

In vain Giles tried to stop the flow, especially as Polly was hovering nearby, an interested listener.

'Now there's a sight for sore eyes!' Molloy blustered, catching sight of Polly. 'Is this your sweetheart, then? And a little beauty, too, if I may say so!'

Polly simpered and came closer. 'I've never met a friend of Giles's before,' she murmured. 'I suppose the two of you knew each other in London, before Giles came here?'

'That we did, my lovely, but until this

minute I never thought to see him again. I thought he gone to sea to fight them Frenchies.'

Polly looked puzzled. 'He told Pa he worked for a fine gentleman in London, who kept a carriage and pair.'

'So he did, my darling, so he did, until the night the press gang took him away. There we were, minding out own business, when they jumped us in a dark alley. Two giants they were, armed with cudgels.'

'And of course you ran off and left me to it,' Giles said bitterly. 'Some friend you turned out to be!'

'I did me best,' Molly insisted. 'I wasn't armed and there was nobody about at that time of night who could help. I couldn't take both of the fellows on, now could I, and you were out for the count. I followed as close as I dared but I had to give up when they threw you into a boat and cast off. If I'd a shown myself I'd have been taking along with you to fight them Frenchies. No doubt you found yourself in the

109

hold of a ship when you woke up, so how did you get away then, eh?'

'Yes, Giles, why don't you tell us all about it?' Polly was watching him closely, and he knew it was only a matter of time before she put two and two together. He laughed uneasily.

'Take no notice of him, Poll! Molloy here was so drunk that night he didn't know which way was up. Not even all the water in the Thames thrown over his addled head would have sobered him up before morning, if then.'

'Not so drunk as I didn't seem them row off with you in the bottom of the boat,' Molloy protested. 'Anyhow, what's it matter who saw what? You got away from the brutes and that's all that matters, eh?'

'Ah, but how and when did he escape, that's what's important,' Polly sneered. 'England is at war with France, Mr Molloy. They don't like deserters, those lords of the navy don't they'll shoot Giles if they catch up with him, or maybe they'll take him back aboard ship and hang him from the yardarm. Isn't that what they call it? I do hope nobody reports him to the authorities!' The expression in her eyes was hard and merciless.

'Here, there's no need for talk like that!' It had finally dawned on Molloy that he had put his foot in his mouth. 'A nice girl like you? You'd never rat on your young man, now would you?'

'Ah, but is he my young man? That's the question, is it not?'

Giles felt sick. He cursed the fates that had brought Barney Molloy to the Angel. His whole future now hung in the balance, or more accurately in Polly's hands. If she still wanted him she might agree to keep quiet, but at what price? He was sure that she would demand that he marry her, and what sort of life would it be if he found himself yoked to a woman he not only did not love, but had come to detest.

'Well, you know my story, so what are you going to do about it?' he asked, looking more confident than he felt. As he spoke, Molloy took the opportunity to slink away once again. Polly looked at Giles without pity.

'I don't know, Giles. You'll just have to wait and see. I'll have to give it some thought, won't I? I will say, though, that it would be a waste of a good man if you swing.' Her insolent gaze swept over him from head to foot before she turned away from him and hurried indoors.

The first person she met in the kitchen was Jemima and she couldn't resist gloating.

'You'll be surprised to know I've discovered your little secret,' she began, helping herself to a cup of tea which Jemima had just prepared for a customer.

'What little secret is that?'

'Why, the one you and my Giles have been hiding from me.'

'I'm hiding nothing, Polly.'

'Possibly that may be true, but he certainly has something he doesn't want anyone to know. He's a deserter from the British navy, which means death if he's caught. When he's caught,' she added.

Jemima's face turned white but she valiantly tried to save the situation. 'I don't know what you're talking about, Polly. I'm sure that Giles has never been to sea. Why, he's always worked with horses, that I do know.'

'You can save your breath,' came the retort. 'I'm going to let Pa know about this. He'll know what we ought to do about it.'

As soon as Polly had left the room, Jemima flew outside to find Giles. The customer would have to wait for her tea; there wasn't a minute to lose.

'She's told you, then,' Giles said flatly, reading the fear and dismay on Jemima's face. 'An old mate from London saw me here and blurted out the story in her hearing. It so happens he was with me the night we were set on by the press gang.'

'Never mind all that! We've got to get away before it's too late. I'll come with you. There may be room for us on the

113

coach, or perhaps your so-called friend will lend you his horse. It's the least he can do after this.'

'I can't take you with me, love. If we're caught, you'll be in trouble too, for aiding and abetting a fugitive. The very least they'd sentence you to is transportation to Botany Bay. I'll go as soon as I can get my things together, and I'll send for you later when I've found a safe place to hide.'

'I don't care. I love you, and I'm not letting you go without me.'

'Nobody is going anywhere!' Jemima swung round to find Eli Bliss looming over her, with a grinning Polly standing in the background, her hands on her hips.

'Get inside, the pair of you; I've something to say.' He grasped her painfully by the arm and although she wriggled desperately he was too strong for her. She was obliged to go where he led and Giles had to follow, having no wish to see her left alone and defence-less.

Eli took them into his private rooms by way of an outside door and Jemima's only consolation was that he quickly put his daughter in her place.

'Get out front at once, girl. There's customers waiting to be served and I don't want them shouting the place down and me losing good money. Get Maggie out of the kitchen if it's too much for you to deal with. What are you waiting for? Go, I say!'

Once inside his parlour, Eli gestured to them to sit down. Jemima perched on the edge of a horsehair sofa, too keyed up to relax. Eli poured himself a glass of Madeira without offering anything to his captives.

'My girl tells me you're a deserter from the navy,' he began.

'I never was in the navy, or not of my own free will,' Giles tried to explain. 'I was taken by the press gang and I got away, that's all.'

'I doubt the lords of the Admiralty would accept that as an excuse,' Eli grunted. 'Once you're in, you're in, no matter how it happened, but that's neither here nor there. The point is that you may be able to help me out of a bit of a jam, and in return I pledge to keep quiet about what I know.'

'And Polly as well?' Jemima spoke up bravely.

'Poll will do as she's told,' he frowned, 'but what about you, miss, hey?'

'Of course I won't say anything!' she smiled at Giles, who managed to grin back.

'I'm talking about you spilling the beans about what I'm going to say next,' Eli corrected, splashing more wine into his glass. 'Oh, I could send you away right now, but how am I to trust your lover here? No doubt the pair of you tell each other everything. So you might as well listen to my plan, on the understanding that if you put a foot wrong at any time your lover dies. I'm not talking about sending him back to the navy, oh, no. I mean that I'll shoot him dead myself, and your life won't be worth a ha'penny bun either. Have I made myself plain?'

'Yes, Master Bliss,' Jemima gulped.

'Very well, then. You have no doubt heard about the highwayman robberies that have been taking place throughout the shire. There are several men involved in this, working under my direction.'

Jemima drew in a quick breath. So she had been right all along!

'This latest robbery has displeased me greatly, for the man who was in my employ has disappeared without turning the proceeds over to me as he was sworn to do. This is a huge loss because he has taken a large amount of gold which was the property of Barclay's Bank and which I had certain plans for.'

'So that is why Polly went away,' Jemima murmured under her breath, 'to carry word to one of the highwaymen that the money was to be on the coach that day!'

Eli glowered at her. 'You'd do well to

look the other way in future, miss. The less you know about my plans the better, as I'm always trying to drum into Polly. Women should never be involved in the affairs of men. They are weak-witted and never to be trusted.'

Jemima managed to avoid answering the insult by clenching her fists inside the pockets of her apron.

'So what is required of me, Master Bliss?' Noticing Jemima's red face Giles thought it was to change the subject.

'You can ride a horse, I suppose?'

'Of course. I was brought up on a farm.'

'No of course about it. There's hundreds of London lads who don't know one end of a horse from the other. An excellent rider, are you? Able to stick on a horse's back when it's in full gallop? Maybe shoot a pistol while you're about it?'

Giles nodded. Unable to keep still for another moment, Jemima jumped up and stared Eli Bliss full in the face.

'You're asking him to hold up

coaches and steal from people, isn't that it?'

Eli sneered unpleasantly. 'Well, I'm not asking him to take part in the Grand National, girl!'

'Giles, you can't!' Jemima was almost weeping as she turned to face her sweetheart.

She was amazed to see that he was leaning back in his chair, looking pleased with himself. Was he bluffing, to put Eli off the scent?

'I'd like to give it a try, Master Bliss. The idea of robbing the rich to help the poor rather appeals to me.

'I suppose you want me to take the place of the ungrateful employee who has made off with the proceeds of your latest venture.'

What on earth was he talking about? Every little boy liked to play Robin Hood with a wooden sword and a feather in his hat, but helping the poor? She stared at Giles, who refused to meet her gaze.

Eli stared at him, looking suspicious.

'I hope you mean what you say, my lad. It would be a clever man indeed who could pull the wool over my eyes! And if you have any thoughts of riding off into the sunset, with or without my money, just bear in mind that I have a little hostage here.

'If you want to see your sweetheart with her throat cut from ear to ear, just try double crossing me.'

'You can count on me, Master Bliss,' Giles assured him,

'When do you want me to start?'

'All in good time, lad. In the meantime, you can get out here and help Polly, my girl. I've finished with you here.'

Jemima shot an agonised look at Giles, who pretended not to notice. Eli came up to her and took her chin in his hand, squeezing painfully.

'Just you remember, Miss, that what is sauce for the goose is sauce for the gander.'

'I don't know what you mean, Master Bliss.'

'Oh, but I think you do! There are

two hostages here, so if you have any thought of sending a message somewhere when the coach leaves, or even travelling on it yourself, it will be the worse for Giles Morton!'

Jemima nodded, feeling sick.

9

Jemima went about her work with her thoughts in a whirl. She managed to upset one customer by bringing her a cup of chocolate instead of the tea that had been requested, and she found herself snapping at Maggie quite un-intentionally.

'My, my, somebody got out of bed on the wrong side this morning,' Maggie observed. 'Didn't you sleep well?'

'I didn't sleep at all. I was far too upset for that.'

'Ah, you're worried about young Giles, of course, this being his first time out. He'll come back safely, don't you fret.'

'So you know what's going on, then.' It was a statement, not a question. Maggie opened her eyes wide in surprise.

'Of course I do. Not stupid, am I?

When you've worked here as long as I have, you don't miss much. The master knows I know, but he trusts me, what with me being his cousin.'

'The master is your cousin!' This would never have occurred to Jemima, but now that she thought about it she could see some resemblance in the set of the jaw, and the large hooked noses that both of them had.

'Bless you, yes. Our mothers were sisters, and when I fell on hard times, Eli offered me a job here. I used to have a little pastry shop of my own, but that man of mine drank away all the profits and there was no point in keeping it up.'

'But why don't you live in?' Jemima wondered. 'The Angel has plenty of empty rooms and it would save you paying rent elsewhere.'

'Eli owns the little cottage where we stay, and besides, if anything ever went wrong with his little sideline, we'd be tarred with the same brush when the authorities came around poking their noses into what don't concern them. On top of that it's best that my man don't be on hand all round the clock with ears flapping or he might let slip something he shouldn't when the drink loosens his tongue.'

'He must be a trial to you,' Jemima murmured.

Maggie sighed. 'He is that. What I ever saw in him I can't tell you. Eli has offered more than once to solve the problem for me, but I stick at murder.'

Jemima suppressed a shudder. If the master could think of killing his cousin's husband, he would have no compunction in eliminating a little chambermaid who failed to do as she was told.

She had to watch her step, yet now that Maggie was in a talkative mood it would be a good time to get her to answer a few questions.

'I don't understand why the master had to send Giles out today,' she began.

'It's common knowledge, he's a man short since that fool Thomas thought he could line his own pockets and run. He did a bad day's work when he decided to double cross Eli Bliss! England will be too small to hold him now. Eli will track him down and he'll get what he deserves.'

'What I meant was, why Giles? Why not Paul Bell? I know he's back. Surely it would have been better to send out an experienced man?'

Maggie stared at her. 'Paul Bell! Why in the world would the master pick on him?'

'But I thought . . . '

'Then you thought wrong! I've told you before, he's not in on that side of things.'

'Then what is he doing here?'

But before Maggie could say more the door opened and Polly swayed into the room.

'Wash going on?' she demanded. 'Talking behind my back, ain't yer?'

'You've been into the port, haven't you, miss? You'd better not let your Pa catch you. You know he don't approve of females drinking.'

'Who cares 'bout him? He sent my Giles out on the road and if anything bad happens I'll never forgive . . . '

She sank down on a nearby chair, mumbling away to herself.

'We can't let her go out there talking like this,' Maggie sniffed. 'Best take her to her room and tell Eli the wench has a headache, which is no word of a lie, if I'm any judge. No, better yet, he'll have to know, and if she gets a whipping once she's sober, that's her lookout, not mine.'

Jemima took Polly by the arm and tried to get her to stand up, but the girl pulled away angrily, shouting that Jemima was to blame for everything. Maggie shoved her back on the seat, none too gently for there was no love lost between her and her cousin's daughter.

'Get out of there and fetch Eli,' she panted. 'Go on, girl, don't just stand there like Simple Simon in front of the pie stall!'

'Don't bother me now, girl,' Eli growled, when Jemima timidly told him that he was needed in the kitchen on a matter of urgency. 'Can't you see I'm busy? Whatever it is will have to wait.' But she stood her ground and he marched into the kitchen, his face turning purple when it realised what the matter was.

'She'll have to be locked in her room, and you'll have to help me with her,' he ordered Jemima. 'We'll have to go round by the outside. The customers mustn't hear her talking like this.'

Thick as the old walls were, Polly's drunken roars penetrated the outer rooms when she found herself locked in. She was only making things worse for herself and Jemima trembled to think what would happen to her when Eli got his hands on her after she sobered up.

Busily serving customers she managed to make out the words 'Giles' and 'love' as did the grinning men at the bar.

'Having a bit o' trouble with your girl, are you, Eli? Sounds like she's locked in back there.' This from one of the locals who knew Polly well. Eli was equal to the occasion.

'Fallen in love with an unsuitable young chap. You know what girls are like. I've sent him off with a flea in his ear and she's letting the world know how she feels about that. Take no notice. She'll come to her senses by the time I've finished with her.'

'Too bad though if she loves the chap.'

'It's nothing that a good pasting won't cure,' Eli replied, his eyes cold.

Jemima wondered if she herself could be cured so easily. Her love for Giles had taken a severe blow when he had ridden off with such a cocky expression on his face. He seemed to be looking forward to what lay before him as an adventure, heedless of the risks involved.

Worst of all, he didn't seem to care that what he was doing was wrong, a criminal offence! People who experienced a hold up on the highway could be affected for life if they happened to be of a sensitive nature, and that aspect of it was worse than the actual loss of their valuables. She knew how she would feel it if ever happened to her.

Despite all this, the flame of her love for Giles Morton burned brightly, even while it flickered slightly. She could understand now how Maggie stayed by her drunken husband, and why Polly couldn't let go of her feelings for Giles, even after he'd made it plain that he didn't care.

Eli Bliss had them all in his toils, like some gigantic spider at the centre of a web.

'Where will it all end?' she asked herself, dabbing at her eyes with the corner of her apron. 'Where on earth will it all end?' If she could have foreseen exactly how it would end she might have pulled her apron over her head and gone into hysterics, but for the moment there was nothing more to be done.

Jemima's worst fears came true when

Giles staggered into the kitchen, covered in blood. She gave a shriek which caused Maggie to drop the pan she was holding, splashing broth all over the table.

'What did you want to go and do that for?' the cook demanded. 'Now see what you've made me do!' but when she turned round and saw Giles clinging to the door frame her normally rosy cheeks became as white as his.

'Sit down here, lad and let me have a look at you. Jemima, bring hot water and towels right away. Don't stand there gawping!'

Jemima did as she was told, although her legs threatened to give way under her. The next half an hour was the longest of her life, although it was Maggie who bravely dug out the ball from his shoulder while issuing orders to both her helper and the victim.

Jemima's main job was to run Eli for a tankard of rum, which Giles needed little persuasion to gulp down. Fortunately there were no customers about because no coach was due until later in the day.

'He's bleeding like a stuck pig,' Jemima wailed. 'Can't we do something to stop it?'

'Not yet,' Maggie answered, through stiff lips. 'Best to let the badness flow away first.' It seemed to Jemima as if her sweetheart's life might seep away along with the 'badness' whatever that was, but by tensing all her muscles she managed to keep quiet.

Eli watched dispassionately as Maggie did her work. 'What happened, man?' he barked. 'I have to know!'

'They were expecting me,' Giles whispered. 'Man with a pistol.' Then he lapsed into unconsciousness.

'He's not dead yet!' Maggie panted. 'Just fainted, or maybe it's the rum. Anyway, it's good that he's out of it for a bit. Get more hot water, girl, and start cleaning him up. We'll have to get him into his bed and we don't want the other lads to see him like this, or it'll start them talking.'

131

'They'll have seen too much already, when he fell off his horse,' Eli snarled. 'We'll have to get him upstairs into one of those empty rooms on the top landing. I'll think up some tale to tell the lads. I already spun them a yarn about giving him time off to visit an old aunt on her deathbed, and they swallowed that easily enough.'

'So they might have,' Maggie huffed, 'but that wouldn't account for him being shot.'

'You just leave that to me. I might have known the young fool wasn't up for the job! Careless, getting himself shot his first time out! I've a good mind to turn him over to the law, let them think he was acting on his own.'

'You can't do that!' Jemima cried.

Eli rounded on her, his great fist raised. 'You don't tell me what I can and can't do, girl! You keep your mouth shut, like I told you before.'

'She's got a point, though,' Maggie cut in. 'He's been working here for months. Those fellows aren't stupid.

You hand him over to them and it'll point them directly to you. They'll take this place apart stone by stone, and where will you be then?'

Eli pondered this for a long moment. 'There is another way. It's a pity you didn't let him bleed to death, our Mag. We could have dumped him in a ditch miles away and that would have been that. Still, it's not too late for that.'

Maggie drew herself up to her full height. 'I've told you before, Eli Bliss, I won't be a party to murder. Just you remember that there's some of us who know more about you than you want known, and you can't put all of us out of the way!'

Jemima held her breath while he deliberated this, releasing it only when he ordered her to help him get Giles upstairs. It was hard work, but at last they had him installed in a clean bed in a section of he inn where strangers seldom went. Eli locked the door and pocketed the key. Maggie protested at this.

'We'll have to look in on him from time to time. I shouldn't be surprised if he isn't delirious by the end of the day. Someone needs to sponge him down and keep him quiet.'

'You, girl! You can do that when you've finished work for the day. Until then I'll keep the key where it's safe. You can take turns with our Polly tomorrow, her being sweet on the lad.'

He laughed unpleasantly, probably enjoying the idea that the two girls would see the man they loved suffering on his bed of pain. Jemima spared a thought for the long-dead Mistress Bliss who had given him his only child. Had he once been a tender lover, or had he treated his wife with the same lack of feeling he meted out to everyone else?

Maggie's assessment of Giles' condition proved to be correct, for when Jemima went to his bedside in the early evening she found him burning with fever and muttering wildly.

She sponged him down, and although

he flinched at the touch of the cold water he let her carry on with the task.

'Don't shoot!' he kept whispering and for a moment she felt exasperated with him. The unknown man was probably only trying to protect himself, for Giles had also been in possession of a pistol. It was all a question of who had pulled the trigger first.

She wondered if Giles had had time to do the same thing. As far as she knew he wasn't a violent person. When it came right down to it, would he have been able to wound or kill another human being?

Yet there was a war on, and thousands of men who had never killed anything more than vermin or a game bird were having to do so at this very moment. It was a case of having to kill or be killed.

The next few days were very hard on everyone. Polly and Jemima looked after Giles as best they could, having declared a truce in the face of adversity. He was conscious now, and in spite of all the blood he had lost it appeared that he would live. Maggie had inspected the wound and pronounced it clean, while telling them to keep a close eye on it in case it began to fester.

Then disaster struck. When the last customer of the day had left the Angel, Eli went around closing the shutters and barring every door. He called everyone into his private parlour for a meeting, something which had never happened before. His usual way of carrying on was to issue orders which were expected to be obeyed. There was no room for argument in the running of the inn.

Polly was there, of course, and Jemima, as well as Maggie who had not been allowed to leave for home. To their amazement Paul Bell was also there, a dark, brooding presence which filled Jemima with a nameless dread. The stables hands were not there, and she assumed that they were still being kept in ignorance about what had become of Giles.

Eli had spun them a yarn about how he had been summoned back to his aunt's bedside — she had first rallied but now was finally dying — and he had gone back by coach. Whether or not they believed this was anybody's guess, but they knew better than to question their master.

'It's happened again,' Eli announced. 'There's been another shooting, only this time a passenger is dead, killed by one of my men. He's been wounded as well, and they've got him in gaol, waiting to hang.' He ignored the gasps which followed this news, and went on 'so if he talks, the law will be on our doorstep before we know it, and unless we're very careful, we could all be facing big trouble. So listen to me, and listen carefully. This is what we're going to do.'

10

Jemima and Polly exchanged anxious glances. For once they were in agreement, worried that Eli had plans for Giles which neither of them would like.

'It's highly likely that John Durwood, my man in Ampthill, will talk if he can see any way of escaping the gallows. I know that the authorities are desperate to put an end to the highway robberies, and for that reason they will do everything they can to force him to speak. They may promise him a lesser sentence if he betrays me, or they may lie to him in that regard, which will serve the same purpose in the end. Thus I expect to find the law on my doorstep at any time in the next few days.'

'So what about Giles, Pa?' Polly wanted to know. 'Can we find a safe place to hide him?'

'Giles is the least of my worries. It is in my interest that these premises should not be searched and that is why we need a plan that will not fail. There is something here that must not be found.' He glanced at Paul Bell as he spoke, and some message flashed between them, left unsaid.

'Money and valuables,' Polly pouted. 'Load them on a cart and take them away before the men get here. What can they do when they find nothing suspicious on the premises?'

Her father ignored her. 'We'll let them see Giles in his bed. He looks sick enough in all conscience.'

'No!' Jemima cried. 'You can't let them have him! I won't let you!' Slender as she was, compared with the burly Eli, she presented a picture of a David facing Goliath. Eli could have broken her neck with his bare hands but fortunately he had other things on his mind.

'Women!' he sniffed. 'They never let a man get a word in edgeways! We let it be known that the boy has some disease that's catching, cholera, mebbe. They can't dare go close enough to see his wound and I wager they'll be out of here so fast they won't bother to search the place.'

'It could work,' Maggie said slowly, 'but it means closing down the Angel, of course.'

'What, and lose all my trade?' he blustered.

'Think, man! If we truly had an outbreak of cholera here no passenger would dare come through those doors, much less sample our food and drink! You'll have to divert the coaches to the Falcon's Rest on the upper road. Foregoing a few days' custom will be nothing compared with what you stand to lose otherwise.'

Paul Bell spoke for the first time. 'The woman talks sense, Master Bliss.'

Eli nodded slowly. 'Very well. It's decided.' He stabbed a finger in Jemima's direction. 'You will talk to young Morton and let him know what's expected of him. If anyone looks inside his door that he doesn't know, he's to toss and moan as if he's in dire straits.'

'I will, Sir, but what about the other stable lads? You've told them that Giles has gone away yet he is still here. What will happen when they're questioned by the law?'

'A good point. I'll tell them I lied so as not to cause panic until we knew what his sickness was.'

'How are they going to explain the blood, then? He was covered with it when he arrived.' This from Maggie, who was good at thinking one step ahead.

'Giles said none of them were around when he got here,' Polly said. 'They were all about their work and he was sure nobody was in sight. He turned the horse loose in the yard and staggered into the kitchen. I'm sure he speaks truly.'

'Be that as it may, I'll have words with them and tell them to play the idiot if asked awkward questions. That shouldn't be hard for either of them. Neither one has the sense God gave him.'

'Does anyone know what cholera looks like?' Maggie asked. 'If so many people die from it, it must affect them a bit more than moaning and groaning. Do you get spots, for instance, or vomit?' Nobody seemed to know.

'Typhus, then. We'll call it that, instead.'

'That's jail fever!' Eli snorted. ''Tis well known how that comes from dirty conditions and lice! Once word of that gets out the Angel is finished.'

'The Angel is finished anyway,' Maggie told him brutally. 'If this works they may not be able to pin anything on you this time, but the suspicion will hang over your head for the rest of your days. You'll have to make other plans for yourself after this, and well you know it.'

Giles was still weak, but looking better rested when Jemima looked in later with a bowl of gruel. He groaned when she told him what he was expected to do.

'When they come, Eli will stall them as long as he can, while we get you ready. We'll put hot rocks in your bed to make you sweat, and Maggie is going to find some red stuff to dye your skin to look like a rash. In the later stages of the disease some victims twitch and go into convulsions, and think they're seeing things that aren't there. Do you think you can manage all that?'

'Manage it! I'll be shaking with terror, never mind pretending to twitch! Wouldn't it be better all round if I could just get away somewhere before these police fellows arrive?'

'The master has his reasons,' she assured him. 'Now remember, the fate of all of us is in your hands. You simply have to make this work!' Giles groaned and rolled over.

Nothing untoward happened for two days. Jemima wished that something would happen to take her mind off the situation, short of the investigators actually turning up.

The coaches continued to roll in as before, and the talk was all about the unfortunate gentleman who had been killed.

'A real hero,' one woman said. 'He stood up and let fly with his own pistol, so nobody else on the coach was hurt at all, or robbed of their possessions.'

'More fool him,' her friend retorted. 'If he'd sat still and kept quiet he'd still be alive today, instead of lying cold in his box.'

'Ah, but that's why everyone's calling him a hero. It's because of him they've caught the highwayman and he'll pay for his misdeeds now. The roads will be safe for honest travellers.'

'Until another one pops up,' someone else said.

'Some say as there's a whole gang of them,' a portly man remarked. 'I'm inclined to believe that myself. Where there's one there may be more! If they put this fellow to the rack he'll likely confess everything, and then we'll see what we shall see.'

One of his female listeners gave a little shriek. 'The rack! Oh, surely they don't use that any more, do they?'

'A figure of speech, Madam, merely a figure of speech. There are other ways of breaking down a criminal's resistance, take it from one who knows.'

Nobody asked him how he knew this. For her part, Jemima didn't want to know anything more. Her nerves were jangling, and every time a male stranger entered the Angel she was convinced that their last hour had come. Perhaps men felt this way while waiting to ride into battle; jittery, and uncertain whether they would be able to perform honourably when the trumpets sounded.

For herself, it took every ounce of courage she possessed not to run as far away from the Angel as she could possibly go.

In the afternoon of the second day Eli bolted the doors and closed the shutters, thereby returning the household to a state of siege. A hastily scrawled notice nailed to the main door read, 'Closed. Sickness within. Livery stable as usual.'

That evening Jemima's heart almost stopped beating when a tremendous pounding was heard on the door, while the whinnying and stamping of newly arrived horses could be heard outside.

'I'm coming, I'm coming!' Eli bawled, as he opened the door a crack. 'Who's there?'

'Who do you think is here?' a deep voice responded. 'I'm the driver of the Bedford coach with a load of passengers wanting rest and food. What do you mean by barring the door?'

'Like it says on the notice, we're closed on account of serious illness. Can't you read?'

'No, I can't! And what's that to do with anything? Inns are supposed to stay open all hours.'

'Not when there's typhus inside, they ain't. You'll have to take your lot to the Falcon, unless they want to go to the stables, of course. Plenty of hay and water offered there!'

'Very funny!' the coachman said, but at the magic word 'typhus' he hurried back to stop his passengers getting off, and within a short time the coach could be heard creaking away.

Eli slammed the door shut and shouted to the inmates of the once prosperous Angel. 'False alarm! You can all get back to what you was doing before.'

Once again they all settled down to wait for the confrontation with the law which would come to them as surely as the next day's sun would rise in the East.

11

Jemima was relieved of her cleaning duties for the moment because when there were no guests staying overnight there was no urgency about sweeping and dusting the rooms. However, between fetching and carrying for the landlord and taking her turn at nursing Giles, she was busy enough.

Once again Paul Bell had disappeared so the only occupants of the Angel were Eli and Polly, Giles, Maggie and Jemima. Maggie's husband had nearly frightened them all out of their skins when he came banging and shouting and demanding to be let in.

'We're closed!' Eli bawled, but the man kept battering at the door.

'Tell my wife to come home! I wants my dinner!'

'He won't go away till he gets what he wants,' Maggie said, biting her lip.

148

'Heaven alone knows what he'll say or do when he's like this, with no food to soak up the liquor. You'd best let me go home with him, master. It can't make no difference whether I'm here or not. Nobody in their right mind would suspect me of being a highwayman!'

Jemima smothered a laugh. Despite all her anxieties she loved the idea of roly poly Maggie galloping across the countryside on horseback, brandishing a pistol.

Grudgingly, Eli agreed that Maggie might as well leave. It was either that or admit her fool of a husband to joining their party, and who knew where that might lead?

Not long afterwards there was a muffled rapping at the side door, which Eli opened a crack in order to speak to Jem, one of the stable hands.

'They've come, master. Two of them, armed to the teeth by the looks of them. Just stepped off the coach from up London. They're at the Falcon now, filling their faces, Frank said. They'll be here in no time!'

'Right, you get about your work, lad. You've done nothing, seen nothing, heard nothing. Do you understand me?'

'Yes, sir.'

'Right then, get off and do as I say.'

Jem's cousin, Frank, was in Eli's pay, and he had delivered the warning not so much because of the money he hoped to receive, but out of fear of what would happen to Jem if he failed in his task.

Eli called the two girls to him. 'Right, then! You know what you have to do!'

Jemima fled upstairs. Closing the window in Giles's room she set light to the fire which was already laid in the grate. Before long the room became uncomfortably hot, and the sweat began to stream down both their faces.

'Do we have to go through this palaver?' Giles grumbled. 'I swear I'll fade to a shadow if this keeps up, and I wish you'd open up that window again, at least until we hear the men coming. I can hardly breathe.'

'You know very well why we're doing this,' she reproved him. 'We have to make them believe you're in a high fever.'

'If I'm so hot already, won't they ask why you make matters worse with a fire on a fine summer's day?'

'Maggie said it's the thing to do, sweating the sickness out of the system. Oh, do stop moaning, Giles! Uncomfortable it may be, but anything's better than hanging, surely?'

'Jemima! Where are you, girl? Get down here at once!' The sound of Eli's roaring floated up the stairs and she hurried down to find him standing in the waiting room with two stern looking men who easily matched the landlord in height and girth.

'This here's my chambermaid, Jemima. She'll tell you what you want to know.'

Not exactly what they wanted to know, she thought, grateful that her long skirts covered her knees, so nobody could see how much they were shaking.

'The landlord wants us to believe

that there's grave sickness in the house,' one of them announced, staring at her rudely. 'We want you to confirm that if you can.'

'Oh, yes, sir, it's one of the stable hands. He's been ailing for days now.' She looked sideways at Eli and was relieved to see him giving her a barely perceptible nod. 'He's got typhus, sir. He's real, bad.'

'You're a doctor then, are you, miss?'

Jemima was bewildered. 'No, of course I'm not. As the master just told you, I'm the chambermaid.'

'No, you're not a doctor, so how is it you can name this man's illness with such certainty? I believe he's one of the men we're looking for, and if he's taken to his bed it's only to pull the wool over our eyes.

'Well, that won't work with us, girl.'

'It wasn't me, sir, who said it was typhus. It was Maggie. She's seen it before and she knows the signs.' Jemima launched into a description of typhus and what it could mean to those unlucky enough to contract it, ending with the fact that in some people gangrene could set in towards the end. 'And I think I'm getting it myself, sir,' she finished desperately. I've been looking after Giles and I don't feel well at all this morning.'

'It's strange that the landlord here is the picture of health, then,' the second man said. 'I think we should see this ailing stable hand for ourselves.'

'Fair enough,' Eli said. 'We've nothing to hide. Jemima will take you to the lad's room.'

'He must be a kindly man, your master,' one of the visitors said as she led them up the first flight of stairs. 'Bringing a sickly stable hand into the house like this.'

Jemima rightly supposed that this was said in an attempt to loosen her tongue, so she said nothing. Moments later they were outside the room where Giles lay, and she threw the door open and stepped inside, closely followed by the men from London.

The stench made her gulp. The heat of the room, the unemptied chamber pot, and the smell of rotten meat assailed her nostrils. She had prudently placed some rotten meat in the press and the smell from that added to the impression that some vile sickness lurked in this room.

Giles, pouring with sweat, tossed and muttered on the bed. She prayed that he wouldn't overdo it, but she need not have worried. The two men stepped back hastily and clattered down the stairs.

'For the love of pity open that window!' Giles gasped. 'What on earth did you put in that cupboard, Jemima? The smell is enough to choke a horse!'

'Not yet!' she whispered. 'Try to hold on a bit longer. I want to see what they're doing now. I'll be back as soon as the coast is clear.'

Loud screams were heard when the pair burst into Polly's own bedroom, where she was reclining on the bed, wearing nothing but her shift. After peering under the bed to make sure nobody was concealed there, the two men retreated.

After glancing hastily into a number of empty rooms they announced they were giving up their search.

'I hope you found what you were looking for!' Eli sneered. 'Too bad you can't go and catch some real criminals, instead of coming here disturbing innocent girls and sick servants.'

'Not this time, luckily for you,' he was told, 'but this isn't finished yet, not by a long chalk. You see, we've a little bird in a cage over in Dunstable, and he's started to chirp. He hasn't said much yet, but we'll get it out of him bit by bit.'

'Don't know what you're talking about, man!'

'Then let me put it this way. We have reason to believe that you're the man behind this spate of highway robberies, the brains behind the scheme if you will. One of them's in gaol, another had gone to ground, and a third is lying upstairs. Oh, I don't doubt his illness is real enough, but that don't mean he wasn't robbing before that started.'

Eli said nothing. The second man took up the tale.

'So here's the point, Master Bliss. With all them fellows out of the picture, the robberies should stop, don't you see? That tells us something. Now, if another one was to take place, that might point to queer goings on elsewhere, but I can't see that happening, can you?'

The two men finally left, promising to return, and Jemima rushed up to relieve Giles. She found him on the top landing, hobbling along with the aid of an old walking stick which Polly had found somewhere.

'It's all right, I saw them leave,' he told her. 'I couldn't stay in that filthy hole another minute.'

'You can't come downstairs yet, Giles. For all we know they may be hiding round the corner, meaning to come back and catch us off guard. Take the room next door until I get yours tidied up.'

In his private apartments, Eli Bliss was pacing up and down while his daughter cowered against the wall, afraid of his wrath.

'You heard what they said, Poll. I've got to work out what to do next.'

'We've got to leave at once,' she whined. 'Get out while the going's good. We could get a boat over to Ireland. They'll never find us there.'

'We can't leave before Paul gets back. No, there has to be another holdup. That will confuse them long enough to buy us time. The thing is, who can do it? They've got hold of poor John and that other devil has gone missing.'

'There's still Mark Fitch up in Bedford,' Polly suggested.

'He's gone soft. His old mother found out what he was up to and begged him to quit. I wouldn't put it past her to go to the justices if she thinks he's started up again.'

'Who, then, Pa?'

'There's no help for it. Giles Morton will have to go. His shoulder must have started to heal by now. I'll go and tell him what he has to do.'

Jemima stared at Eli Bliss in horror. 'You can't make him do that! He's not well. He's been shot!'

'It's his left shoulder. Luckily he's right handed. If he's the horseman he pretends to be he can use a pistol and ride at the same time. It won't matter if he doesn't come away with much in the way of money.'

'I won't do it,' Giles said firmly. 'The countryside will be crawling with officers of the law by now. Every stagecoach will have armed men aboard. I'd be killed or captured without a doubt. I've played my part for you, Master Bliss, and got wounded in your service. I'll do no more.'

'And I've done right by you by keeping you in my house and letting the girls take care of you. In return you'll do as I say or I'll turn you over to the authorities. I'll say I was mistaken in thinking you innocent and now, having learned the truth, I'm doing my civic duty by calling in the law!'

Giles stood, meaning to walk away, but he swayed dizzily and sank back into his chair. Jemima rounded on Eli.

'There, you see? He's far too weak to ride! Please, master, think again!'

'Somebody has to go, girl, so unless you want to take his place, then Giles Morton it is!' This was idle talk, of course and nobody was more surprised than Eli Bliss when Jemima stuck out her chin and said that she was prepared to go out to hold up the coach. Giles looked on in amusement, but his expression darkened when he realised that Eli was taking her offer seriously.

'Can you ride a horse, girl?'

'Yes, I can.'

Under normal circumstances a town girl of Jemima's class would not have had this skill, but Aunt Mag had done sewing for a well to do family who lived near Hyde Park. They had a daughter who loved to ride, but when she had gone away to a school for young ladies someone had to exercise her beloved pony, and the animal was too small to bear the weight of one of the grooms.

For a time it was taken out on a leading rein to trot behind another horse, but it needed to be ridden if it was not to lose its good manners. Jemima was asked if she would like to oblige and she gladly did so, spending many happy hours on Snowball's back until Miss Eleanor returned from school.

Jemima had a nasty idea that riding a large, galloping horse would be a far cry from dealing with a gentle pony, but she was prepared to try if it meant saving the man she loved.

Giles tried hard to dissuade her but her mind was made up. As for Eli, he looked on Jemima as expendable.

'You know the horses in my stable, Morton. Which one would do for this little outing, would you think?'

'Molly,' Giles answered at once. 'She's steady, and that's what's needed now.'

'Pshaw! She's not going out for a little trot on Rotten Row! What about Birchwood? He's fast.'

'Of course he's fast! He was used for racing until his owner lost him in a game of chance. You put Jemima on his back and he'll take her all the way to Yorkshire before you have time to turn around. If you won't send Molly then I suggest Tamar. She can turn on a sixpence, she can, and that's important if Jemima needs to get away in a hurry.'

So Tamar it was, and Eli took Jemima away to explain to her what she had to do. She felt strangely calm. All this while she had believed that matters where outside her control, but now that she was actually about to do something she felt better.

* * *

The following evening she found herself having second thoughts, but by then it was too late. There she was, wearing a mask and dressed in black garments, waiting in the shadow of some mighty oaks, mounted on Birchwood, for Eli had broken his promise to Giles. The tall animal had picked up on her anxious mood and was dancing about in circles as Jemima tried in vain to keep him standing in one place.

She berated herself for being such an utter fool. She had let herself in for this stupid exercise in the heat of the moment, but now cold reason had set in and she knew that no good could come of this. She mentally reviewed Eli's instructions.

'The coach should be leaving the Falcon just after dusk. You'll wait at the crossroads and at the last possible minute you'll walk your mount forward and call on the coachman to stop.'

'I suppose I have to say 'stand and deliver', do I?'

'Never mind all that. Fancy words don't count. 'Stop, or I fire' would have more effect in this case.'

'And what if they don't stop? Do I pursue them?'

'Just fire your pistol into the air.'

Jemima had never used a firearm in her life, and she was afraid of the recoil. What if the horse shied when she pulled the trigger and bolted, or worse, reared up and deposited her on the ground?' A fine highwayman, she was going to make..

The only reason she didn't give up there and then was the fact that Eli had stressed it wasn't important that the coach actually be robbed, although if she managed to get away with something of worth, that would be a bonus and she would not find him ungrateful.

Seated on the horse, Jemima stared in the direction from which the coach would come, straining her eyes to catch a glimpse of it. There was a pale moon in the sky over which dark clouds drifted from time to time. All was quiet, and no birds sang.

All of a sudden strong arms grasped her around the waist and she pulled from the horse and thrown to the ground. For one wild moment she hoped that it was Giles, who had somehow managed to come to her rescue, but she was soon disillusioned.

'Don't make a sound and you won't get hurt,' a familiar voice said and she realised that her attacker, who was now holding the frightened horse by the bridle was Paul Bell.

'What are you doing here? What do you want with me?'

'I suppose I owe you some sort of explanation,' he sighed, 'especially as you'll never see me again after tonight.'

Jemima hoped this wasn't a threat on her life, but she knew she mustn't upset him, so she remained still and waited.

'I expect you know that England is at war with France,' he began.

'Of course. Everybody knows that.'

'And you know about the troubles in Ireland?'

'I think so,' she said uncertainly. There had been a rebellion there three years earlier, having something to do with religion and politics, but since she seldom saw a newspaper this news had mostly passed her by.

'I'm working with those who hope to free Ireland from British rule, Jemima. I'm here in England to raise money for the cause and to meet with our supporters. The late Mrs Bliss was Irish, as was his mother, and for their sake he has given me shelter at the Angel where I can work in secret.'

'Oh,' was all Jemima could think of to say. Compared with running a band of criminals who robbed stagecoaches Bell's story paled by comparison, or so she thought. He sensed this from her lack of enthusiasm and began to boast.

'At the time of the rebellion, back in '78, French soldiers landed on the west coast of Ireland, as well as in Donegal. Unfortunately they were beaten back, but make no mistake about it, we shall try again, and soon.'

'French soldiers? I don't understand. Why would Bonaparte want to go to Ireland? I'd have thought he had enough to do as it is, with the war going on.'

'That's exactly it,' Bell said impatiently. 'From certain bases in Ireland the French would be able to land in England with ease and then Bonaparte could fight you English on your own soil, and win! The Irish are willing to help them, and in return we shall be freed from British rule.'

'Then why are you waiting for the stagecoach? Has Eli sent you here to do the job instead of me?'

'This has nothing to do with Eli. I happen to know that this coach is carrying a great deal of money, which I intend to intercept. As soon as I have it I shall return to Ireland and others will decide how it is to be used.'

As he spoke he swung himself up into the saddle and cocked the pistol. Jemima could hear the rumble and rattle of the approaching coach. She knew that there was nothing she could do to stop him but now she had to look after herself. For all she knew he meant to dispose of her here and now; why else would he have felt free to unburden

166

himself to her? Stealthily she crept behind the biggest of the ancient oak trees.

'I regret that I must leave you to make your own way back to the Angel,' he called back over his shoulder, as he led the great black horse into the roadway. The coach came into view, manned by several burly constables who were squashed together on the top. Hardly daring to breathe Jemima put her fingers in her ears and thus missed the shouting and screaming which followed. Her part in the drama was over.

12

Jemima trudged wearily across country, occasionally tripping over some small obstacle when visibility was poor. The wind had come up and clouds darkened the moon. Far away she heard the sound of several shots but she didn't look back. Her feet were beginning to hurt. Her borrowed boots, dew-soaked, were rubbing her heels and she knew she could expect blisters before she reached the Angel.

She had little choice but to keep going. She could, of course, sit down and wait until daylight, when there was certain to be some traffic on the road. Some farm wife, taking goods to market, would no doubt take pity on her and give her a ride, but how could she explain her appearance? Decent young women did not prowl the countryside at night dressed in men's clothing!

All was quiet when she finally limped into the yard at the Angel. Not even the stable hands were about at this early hour. She hoped fervently that Maggie was back; a hot meal would seem like heaven to Jemima in her condition.

She found Eli in his parlour. To judge by his dishevelled appearance he hadn't been to bed. Polly was there, lounging on a chaise; she, too, was fully dressed but she looked like a hen who has been set upon by stronger birds in the farmyard. Her dress was crumpled and her hair was all awry.

'There you are at last, girl! What happened? Did you manage to stop the coach? Is my horse all right?'

'The horse is gone,' she said wearily. How like Eli to care more for his possessions than for the people in his employ! Before he could work himself up into a rage she told him what had happened during the night.

'Paul Bell! I might have known. No matter. Either way this will divert suspicion from me.' He rubbed his hands together thoughtfully.

Jemima no longer cared what he thought. 'How is Giles? Is he all right? I must go up and see.'

'He's not there,' Polly announced, rousing herself slightly at the sound of his name. 'Pa sent him out to the stable after you left.'

Jemima was furious. 'Surely you don't expect him to work with that injured shoulder? It's only half healed. If he does too much the bleeding will start up again.'

'No need to fret,' Eli grunted. 'I just wanted him out of the way in case the law turned up again.'

Jemima turned to Polly. 'Then why aren't you out there seeing to him?'

Polly put her hands up to her face, shaking her head. 'Because I don't care what happens to him, that's why. He was mine, Jemima Coates, until you turned up and after that he never looked my way again. What have you got that I haven't, tell me that!'

This was an old story and Jemima

wasn't prepared to hear any more of it. 'Pull yourself together, Polly,' she snapped. 'Why throw yourself at a man who isn't interested? There's plenty more fish in the sea.'

'That's what I tell her,' Eli muttered, 'but will she listen? If you had a horse that wouldn't run, you'd get rid of it. Sweethearts is the same. Nothing you can do about Giles Morton, my girl, and that's that!'

This roused Polly out of her lethargy. 'That's what you think, Pa. I got my own back on him, all right! How d'you think he got shot, hey?'

Her listeners glanced at her, open-mouthed.

'That's right! When Pa sent me away with a message for Paul Bell I did more than that! I went to the authorities and told them there was due to be a hold-up, and where! That's why they were armed men on the coach, you see. It was too bad that Giles was only wounded. I hoped he'd be shot dead but there, he never causes me anything but disappointment.'

'You rotten traitor!' Eli bawled, fetching her a clout which made her topple to the floor. 'I ought to strangle you with my own bare hands, and 'twould be no more than you deserve! You could bring the law down on me if he'd been taken alive!'

Polly was past caring. 'They've got John anyway. What's the difference?'

Her father delivered another thump, accompanied by foul language such as Jemima had never heard before, even on the streets of London. She now noticed that a small panel in the wall had been pushed aside, revealing a small dark cavity. Was this where Eli kept his ill-gotten gains? He saw her looking and closed it with a snap.

A furious pounding on the Angel's main door made all three of them jump. Suddenly aware that she was still wearing her disguise, Jemima fled upstairs where she pulled off the jacket and breeks and hid them in her bed. As she pulled a cotton gown over her head she heard shouting down below and she tiptoed to the top of the stairs to see what was going on.

Two burly men had Eli in a firm grasp, while two more were attempted to subdue Polly, who was kicking and screaming. Even she became quiet when she heard what was said next. A tall, quiet man, who seemed to be in charge, was explaining why they had come, and what was to happen next.

'You're man in the Dunstable gaol has spilled the beans, good and proper,' he remarked.

'Don't you take no notice of him!' Eli spat. 'He always was a liar. Betray his own grandmother if it suited him, that one would.'

'Let's just say he prefers not to hang. He's turned King's Evidence and he'll be sentenced to transportation to Botany Bay instead, in return for telling us what we wanted to know.'

'There you are, then. This proves it, don't it? He'd say anything to save his own skin!'

The officer of the law ignored this. 'Take him away, lads. Keep a firm grip on him, mind. We can't let this one get away!'

'Pa, oh, Pa!' Polly snivelled. 'What about me? What am I supposed to do now?'

Eli remained silent while handcuffs and shackles were fastened on to his wrists and ankles.

'You can come along with us,' the officer told her, not unkindly. 'Or you can stay here if you'd rather. We'll be coming back to do a thorough search of the place after we get your father safely under lock and key. In the meantime, is there anything you'd like to tell us?'

Shrinking back behind the newel post, Jemima held her breath. Would Polly betray Giles yet again? Would she give them the details of how Jemima herself was involved? She had helped to hide Giles, she had been aware of what Eli Bliss was up to, not to mention Paul Bell! And what about last night's little exploit?

It hardly mattered that she had not held up the coach after all; her intentions had been dishonourable. She wondered what the penalty for these crimes might be. Perhaps none of it amounted to a hanging offence but she would certainly be shipped away to perform years of hard labour in some penal colony on the other side of the world.

But all the fight had gone out of Polly and she shook her head. She followed the little parade of men outside. Running to a window, Jemima saw Eli and Polly being pushed into a coach, accompanied by their captors. Several more men were seated on the outside. Slowly the coach moved off. Jemima began to shake. It was over.

'Where is he? Where's Giles?' Jemima demanded. Strangely, everything seemed normal in the stables. Horses were placidly eating their morning rations, and the two stable hands were doggedly going about their work, seemingly oblivious to the drama which had just played out inside the Angel.

'Up here!' a voice called down, and she glanced up to see him peering out of the hay now. 'Is it safe to come down?'

'Stay where you are. I'll come up. I've got a lot to tell you!'

Enveloped in a hug which took her breath away, Jemima relaxed for the first time in many hours. She hardly knew where to start. She began by telling him about Paul Bell, trying to make sense of what he had told her about the Irish situation, but the only part that interested Giles was that Bell had come on the scene before it was too late.

'I was half out of my mind with worry, especially when the lads told me you'd gone out on Birchwood. Even if you escaped being shot by someone on the coach, I could see you lying somewhere with a broken neck!'

'Never mind all that. The question is, what do we do now? Those men are coming back, and they mustn't find us here.'

'We could take a couple of horses and ride off. I think I could manage one-handed.'

'We can't risk it. Polly may change her mind when she's had time to mull things over and she might betray us. They'll be on the lookout for a man and a girl leaving this district. There's a cart here, isn't there? We could load it up with hay and hide you in that. I'll drive, and if anyone tries to stop me I'll say I'm a farm girl, making a delivery or something. None of those officers are local men, so they'll be none the wiser.'

'I suppose it could work,' Giles said doubtfully.

'We have to try it. What other choice do we have?'

They sat for a moment without speaking, and then Giles frowned. 'We can't just wander the roads without a definite plan in mind, Jemima. We must have a proper destination. What would you think of going to Bedford, to your uncle? We could hide there for a time until the hue and cry dies down, and they'd never suspect we'd go right into the lion's den, the town where they'll be holding Eli and the rest.'

Jemima gasped. 'Are you mad, Giles Morton? My uncle would as soon shelter us as take a bunch of Frenchies under his roof!' Had it not been that the situation was so serious she would have laughed out loud. The idea of stern, upright Joshua hiding two criminals was quite unthinkable, even if one of them was his own niece!

'Do you have a better idea, then?'

'I suppose there's Mistress Wainwright at Meppershall. We might try her.'

'Who?'

'She's someone I met when I first arrived here. She told me I could go to her if I was ever in trouble. I'd trust her before I would my uncle.'

'That might work for you. After all, she's not to know what you've been up to. You can play innocent and she'll believe you. Tell her the work was too hard, or the male customers too rough, something like that. But what about me? How do you explain a wounded man when the whole shire knows about the highway robberies and the rest of it? And how long is it going to be before the news gets out about Eli Bliss and the goings on at the Angel? Your old friend won't be so pleased to know you then!'

They argued the point back and forth until at last Jemima jumped up in dismay and said that if they didn't get as move on the law men would be back and catch them.

'Can you get the lads to load hay on to that cart, and hitch up a suitable horse? I must go over and gather up my things.'

Giles heaved himself to his feet as Jemima nimbly climbed down the ladder. Her few bits and pieces were important to her, but there was something else she wanted to do before leaving the Angel for good.

First she went to her room to pack, which was the work of just a few minutes. Then she went to the kitchen to gather up as much food as she could carry. A large pork pie, two loaves of bread, getting stale, and a few withered apples from last autumn's harvest. It was not very exciting fare but who knew when they would be able to buy more?

They wouldn't dare to go into taverns or shops, and indeed it might be necessary for them to hole up by day and travel the roads at night. Two pewter mugs completed her haul; with any luck they could drink from streams they found along the way. She stuffed all this into a sack.

After peering out of the door to make sure that the coast was still clear, Jemima tiptoed into Eli's parlour, suffering a bad case of the jitters as she did so, despite the fact that he was certainly not there to pounce on her. She opened the panel without difficulty and soon was examining a pile of small leather bags, most of which contained money, a great deal of it in fact.

Stifling her conscience she took up as

many of these bags as she could carry, taking a moment to see what was in the rest. It was a veritable pirate's treasure. Rings, gold pocket watches, brooches sparkling with jewels, pretty necklaces and heavy chains met her astonished eyes.

These she would leave for the other searchers to find, and perhaps these items would eventually be restored to their rightful owners. She had never forgotten the tearful woman who had been so distressed at losing her late mother's brooch.

Staggering under the weight of the sack, Jemima went to join Giles who was already seated in the cart. She prudently bestowed a golden guinea on each of the table lads, whose eyes opened wide at the sight of so much wealth.

'Be careful when you try to spend it, mind,' she cautioned them. Their nods and winks assured her that they understood.

'I've been thinking,' Giles said. 'We'll

spend tonight at Meppershall, only I'll hide somewhere nearby. After that we'll travel west until we reach Wales. We'll be safe there. I've heard tell that the Welsh think little of those who keep the law for the English justices. We'll be married as soon as we cross into Wales, my love.'

'I'll think about it,' Jemima laughed, as she drove the cart out of the stableyard, knowing that Giles was safely hidden under the hay. Of course she had every intention of doing as he said, for she wanted to keep him at her side for the rest of her life, but it wouldn't do to seem too eager. Men needed to be kept in suspense occasionally. It was good for them.

She looked back at the Angel for the last time. Her stay there was already taking on the semblance of a dream. She thought of the sack that was lying beside her lover.

The money would keep them in comfort for a long time to come. For a moment she felt badly about having stolen it from Eli, who for all his evil ways had provided her with a job and a roof over her head, but then she shook her head. He wouldn't be needing it where he was going, would he?

She clicked her teeth at the horse, who broke into a trot. Joyfully, Jemima began to sing. She was travelling on to a happy future with the man she loved, and what more could she ask of life?

THE END